Praise for Jeff Parker's novel *Ovenman*:

The Taste of Penny

The Taste of Penny

stories

Jeff Parker

DZANC
BOOKS

DZANC
BOOKS

1334 Woodbourne Street
Westland, MI 48186
www.dzancbooks.org

These stories have appeared in the following journals and anthologies:

"An Evening of Jenga®" as "The Tower" in *Pindeldyboz*; "The Back of the Line" in *Hobart*; "Bingo" in *The Mississippi Review*; "The Boy and the Colgante" in *The Best of the Web 2009* (Dzanc Books), *Waccamaw*, and *For Crying Out Loud* (Ferno House Press); "The Briefcase of the Pregnant Spylady" in *Columbia* and *Unsquared: Ann Arbor's Edgiest Writers* (826Michigan); "False Cognate" in *Best American Nonrequired Reading 2006* (Houghton Mifflin), *Stumbling & Raging: More Politically Inspired Fiction* (MacAdam Cage), and *Hobart*; "James's Fear of Birds" in *CutBank*; "James's Love of Laundromats" in *Panhandler*; "James's Low Moment" in *The Journal*; "The Taste of Penny" in *Ploughshares* and *The Robert Olen Butler Prize Stories 2005* (Del Sol Press); "Our Cause" in *Indiana Review*; "Two Hours and Fifty-three Minutes" in *Four Letter Word: New Love Letters* (Simon & Schuster); "Owned" in *Phoebe*. All the James stories also appeared in the chapbook *The Back of the Line* published by DECODE with art by William Powhida.

Published 2010 by Dzanc Books
Book design by Steven Seighman

06 07 08 09 10 11 5 4 3 2 1
First edition April 2010

ISBN-13: 978-0-9825204-4-4

Contents

False Cognate   11

Our Cause   26

The Taste of Penny   48

An Evening of Jenga®   69

The Boy and the Colgante   79

The Briefcase of the Pregnant Spylady   88

Owned   102

James Stories

    James's Fear of Birds   107
    The Back of the Line   112
    James's Low Moment   120
    James's Love of Laundromats   132

Bingo   146

Two Hours and Fifty-three Minutes   160

for Mom and Bruce

False Cognate

WHEN I FIRST ARRIVED HERE, I HAD A SIMPLE request of our liaison, a handsome, tall woman with steel-blue eyes and a pancake face. I wasn't yet confident in my Russian and needed a haircut. I asked her, in English, "Do you know, Tanya, where I can get a barber? I heard they go for about thirty rubles here."

She looked at me with a rather sharp glance and said, "Thirty rubles is one dollar."

"About what my last one was worth," I said, mussing up my hair.

"That's not for me to judge," she said. "The best thing to do is wait at the bus stops. They'll come up to you."

"Come up to me?" I said.

"Eventually," she said.

"That's how people go about it?"

"I think so," she said, then clip-clopped away.

I spent the better part of a week hanging out at the bus stops trying to look like I wanted a haircut. The only people who ever approached me were thin-lipped prostitutes.

Tanya avoided me after that. The whole cohort avoided me. At first I thought they were just an unsociable bunch, but sometimes, walking home at night, I'd see them all at the beer garden near my flat, laughing and having a good time. I'd pull up a chair and they'd suddenly evacuate. Later on, I convinced this Spanish guy who considered himself a Defender of Women to tell me why everyone hated me, and he said word got around that I had showed up the first day and asked the program liaison where I could find a whore. He added that I was what was wrong with Americans and didn't I have a sister and—poking me in the chest with his finger—how would I feel if his Spanish ass came over to America expressly to fuck her?

I couldn't figure out what he was talking about, but he looked like he was going to hit me. I left.

I gave it some thought, and the only explanation was that she'd mistaken the English word *barber* for the Russian word *baba*—a funny thing because I had a history with the word *baba*. I had written a prize-winning essay for my upper-level Russian Composition class in which I'd identified a flaw in an acclaimed Babel translation. Babel had a situation in which a simple young peasant girl, referred to as a *baba*, strolls into a bar drawing all the men's attention. The word *baba* has three meanings: *plumpish old woman, simple young peasant girl*, and, in slang, *whore*. The translator had rendered it as an old haggard babushka, which didn't make any sense. Why would the men find their attention inexplicably drawn to her, except for her hideousness, which wasn't the point at all? I found the original, identified the problem, and composed the essay, winning the prize.

Since *barber* is not a common English word and our liaison's English was about as good as my Russian, she could only hear a Russian approximate. False cognate. This was the only explanation. It works the other way too. When Russians, in the course of normal conversation, describe a lecture as exciting and inspirational the Russian word for which is *pathetichiske*, I hear only *pathetic*. At the kiosks late at night, young men ask for *preservativi* and I'm imagining cured pears when it's the Russian word for *condoms*; when I hear *narciss* on the lips of a young woman strolling through the garden with her lover my immediate mind thinks *self-involved prick* when it somehow means *daffodil*.

For a couple days, I tried to set the record straight. I spoke to Tanya about it. "Why do you think I was mussing my hair while I asked you? What do *babas* have to do with hair?" She clearly didn't believe me. I spoke to others in the cohort as well. "Like from my essay?" I said, "The one that won the prize? Imagine the irony!"

No one believed me.

So I was there with a group and by myself at the same time.

It turned out to be the best thing going for me.

While the others dance a vodka-tainted Merengue at a club called Havana Nights, I wash my socks in a bathroom designed so that you have to straddle the toilet to take a shower.

While the others are in classes, I check out the obscure museums, see Rasputin's actual penis and Peter the Great's collection of deformed babies, which float in jars like smooth balls of fresh mozzarella. I live the real Russian life: isolated, feet wet, maligned.

And on weekends they check the city of fountains or the Tsar's Summer Palace or sun themselves bare- and flabby-assed on the rocky beach at the Peter and Paul Fortress. I take the bus to the provinces.

The Novgorod bus is late so I sit at the beer garden in the courtyard of my building and read the newspaper. Lena is sitting there with a friend, dark-skinned, maybe Tajek or Azerbajani. Lena hates me too. She hates me because I pee behind her office, a wooden shed with a keg inside it. My bladder is worthless and five minutes after a beer, I have to go. All the Russian guys go back there and so I do too.

Lena doesn't like this, but the only option is to take the eight flights of stairs to my apartment and stand in the shower to pee.

Lena, who doesn't think much of my Russian, says to her friend, "Take this goat, Choika. He doesn't speak a word of Russian, and he pees behind this box every day."

I buy a bottle of beer and some dried squid from her.

"You're very beautiful," I say in my admittedly heavily-accented Russian. "Three words in Russian. Oh, look at that—seven, eleven." She spits over her shoulder.

Lena *is* very beautiful, but her friend even more so. I watch them over the top edge of the newspaper and when they look, drop my eyes to some paragraph: *Sergei V. Yastrzhembsky, Putin's senior advisor on Chechnya, suggests that Islamic extremists co-opt the Black Widows against their will to*

become suicide bombers. "Chechens are turning these young girls into zombies using psychotropic drugs," Mr. Yastrzhembsky said. "I have heard that they rape them and record the rapes on video. After that, such Chechen girls have no chance at all of resuming a normal life in Chechnya. They have only one option: to blow themselves up with a bomb full of nails and ball bearings."

Choika stands up. She is wearing a half-shirt and there's a square Band-Aid displayed prominently on her hip. It looks like a nicotine patch, but the guide at the Erotica Museum who showed me Rasputin's penis said that they're the new fashion in birth control.

Choika and Lena hug each other and cry. Then Choika scurries across the street to where the bus has pulled into the station. I chug the rest of my beer and run after her.

The driver stands outside the bus smoking and collecting tickets. "Nice shoes," he says to me. He's in New Balance sneakers identical to mine. It's obvious mine are authentic and his are the imitations you buy in the market. Already the threads along the tongue are pulled and loose. The rubber sole is separating. USA is embroidered on both our heels. "How much?" he says.

"They're my only shoes."

"It's okay. Not a problem."

Ahead of me in line, two babushkas lecture Choika on the length of her skirt. She tells them it's the fashion. They say something about she won't be welcome in Novgorod like that. She says in her opinion she'll be very welcome.

I watch her shoes, white strappy things with heels like icepicks, and wonder why it is I think the word *babushka* rather than *old lady*. It comes easier than other words. I wonder when I'll think *devushka* instead of *girl*. I want to think *devushka* instead of *girl*.

I grab the last seat across from Choika and the two babushkas, next to two passed-out soldiers. I smile at Choika. She clutches her bag and looks out the window.

The driver stands on the steps at the front of the bus and shouts, "Attention, attention. I am very sorry to report that the bathroom on this bus is out of order today. In light of this unfortunate development we will be stopping once or twice whenever the possibility for a bathroom opportunity presents itself."

The soldier to my left comes to. He reaches across the aisle and puts his hand on Choika's stockinged knee. "Oh Caucasian beauty," he says.

The babushkas bang their canes against the seats.

"Relax my friends," the soldier says. He removes his hand from her knee and puts it on mine. Choika never looks away from the window.

"Do you know the game Submarine?" he asks me.

"I've heard," I say. The game is very popular among students. I had heard of those in my cohort playing. But no one was inviting me.

From what I gather a kind of game master they call Captain locks a group of friends in a flat with several bottles of vodka and some pickles. They cannot bring watches, and all clocks are unplugged. The telephone and television are removed by the Captain and no cell phones are permitted. He locks them in the flat and goes about his life, taking the key. The players block the light from all the windows and drink, sleep, drink, sleep, eat pickles, drink, sleep, etc. They

are not allowed to peek out the window or stop drinking while they are awake. Two days later the Captain returns and lets them out.

He smiles at me. "We have been operating Submarine for ten days."

"It's a long time," I say.

"Our Captain—he forgot about us."

With his hand still on my knee, the soldier falls asleep again.

"You are giving away so much," the babushka whispers to Choika.

"Much or not much," Choika says.

I play out this fantasy: Choika is one of the Black Widows from the article.

And it makes a lot of sense. Her eyes never flinch. Even when the bus slams into potholes, she stares steadily out the window. Her bag is not quite big enough for luggage yet larger than an ordinary purse, the perfect size to conceal a wad of nails and ball bearings. She is just old enough to have had a young husband who died recently in the war.

How would she know Lena then? That was the hole...Unless Lena's family, hard up for money like most Russian families, had become Chechen sympathizers purely out of financial necessity, taking in Black Widows, housing them, feeding them, taking care of them while plotting out the best, most populated, most unexpected routes. That was how they managed to buy that box with the keg in it where they sold dried squid and preservativi. I look around the bus. It's packed.

I kind of get-off on this idea. I can already imagine the cutline on the national news back home: Black Widow suicide bomber blows up bus outside of St. Petersburg, Russia. One American is among the dead.

My life reduced to that one line. I lean across the seat to Choika and whisper, "Your way is fraught with peril; your plight, an admirable one."

She does not turn her head.

"Devil," the babushka says, crunching on sunflower seeds. "Now you've got foreigners drooling."

I disturb the soldier's hand from my knee and he jumps to his feet, wobbling slowly into the aisle and teetering to the back of the bus.

The driver, looking up at us from a rear-view mirror the size of an ironing board, yells at him. "Hey, jerk," he says. "The bathroom is out of order."

"I'll piss the floor then," the soldier says.

The driver swings the bus onto the shoulder, knocking the soldier down. The brakes are still hissing and the driver is up, halfway down the aisle. The other soldier grabs his arm as he goes by.

"Reconsider any manly-man," the other solider says.

"No," the driver says, "nothing like that." The soldier in the aisle crawls to his feet again and lights a cigarette. "Friends," the driver says, "let me talk to you then, outside. Everybody, let's take a bathroom break."

"Where are we supposed to go?" a woman shouts from the back. "Under some death cap?"

"Find a nice tree," the driver says.

Choika stands up. I think, *detonation*.

"I believe someone asked you kindly, sir," she says.

"Where exactly are women supposed to go?"

"I believe someone answered, miss. There's some congenial trees in the area," the driver says. "They're cleaner than most bathrooms. You have five minutes or we leave without you."

"And what about ticks?" one of the babushkas says.

"Make sure you get their heads," the driver says.

The babushkas break out some toilet paper and sell squares for two rubles each. Choika buys two. The passengers disperse into the forest. I hold it and eavesdrop. The soldiers and driver stand around a rock talking. There is a lot of nodding but I can't hear them. The soldiers deliberate between one another and say something back to the driver. Then they all shake hands and pee together on the rock.

I go towards what I think is Choika's tree. Another woman I don't recognize steps out and yells at me for sneaking up on her. I use her tree after she's gone and when I'm done Choika and the soldiers are back on the bus and the driver is beeping.

I take the small portion of the seat the soldiers leave me. The soldier who'd kept his hand on my knee holds out his hand, this time to shake. "Andre Andrevich," he says. "Let me guess: Fritz?"

"American," I say.

"Even better," he says, scooting over to give me more room. "Share some beer with us." He takes a warm bottle from his duffle bag and hands it to me. "The danger in playing Submarine is in the doors. Russian doors are the problem, but, well, let's say you don't have to worry about them when you have a responsible Captain. Our Captain was also interested in drinking. And one of the rules of Submarine—strictly enforced by players—is that you cannot look out the window and you cannot know the time, and as a consequence you never know how long you've been playing."

"You don't get light through the crevices?" I ask.

"You get, which is why you tape the curtains to the wall with electrical tape."

The other soldier knocks on the window to get Choika's attention. She is like a statue, a perfect flesh statue with a birth control patch on her hip. The other soldier hunkers down in his seat to try and see up her skirt.

"You should be in Submarine for two days, but sometimes time goes slow and sometimes fast. We think it was the sixth day when we realized, perhaps time was going too slow."

"It seems impossible to me, to mistake six days for two," I say.

"Luckily, we had good amounts of vodka, and pickled garlic."

He replaces my beer and takes the empty. He puts the empties on the floor and says, "Watch this." He points at his watch. The babushkas set these newspaper hats full of sunflower seeds on the seat and pick up the empties. They drop them in plastic sacks and go back to eating their seeds. "Five seconds," he says, "a new record."

"You're throwing away money," one of the babushkas says. "You could use a manicure, but you are not accurate."

"You cannot hear through Russian doors," Andre says. "We were shouting. We thought we would die there. We were pounding on the doors, but this is like a mouse running on a pipe. We were on the top floor, Vadim screaming for help out the windows. Everyone thought we were just drunk."

"We were fucking drunk," Vadim, the other soldier, says.

"When the Captain finally arrived he tried to tell us that it had only been two days. I told him, 'Prepare to suffer' and he admitted that he had forgotten us, and he confessed—you will never believe this: He had been off playing Submarine himself. He was a player in two other games of Submarine before he remembered about us. Since he didn't shower, he didn't find the key in his pocket. He also lost our cell phones."

I tell Andre my story about "barber" and "baba," which he laughs at once I explain that in English a "barber" is someone who cuts hair. He elbows Vadim and tells him my story. He and Vadim crack up.

"Let me tell you," Andre says, "*all* women are whores."

"Watch your mouth," one of the babushkas says.

"I've written an essay about this phenomenon," I say to Andre. "It was awarded a very prestigious collegiate prize in the US."

Choika sits like a statue. Her bag in her lap, her legs crossed official-like. She hardly jostles. I am more and more disappointed that she has not blown us all up. I contemplate peeing into an empty beer bottle. Instead I set the bottle on the floor and one of the babushkas snatches it.

The cops pull over our bus and the driver calls another bathroom break to deal with them. I am happy for the bathroom break, the first one off the bus. I whiz behind the wheel and climb back aboard before everyone else is even off. The cops and the driver are talking near the front of the bus, and I see the driver hand them some money.

Choika steps off the bus and walks around the cops

and the driver. I hurry back to my seat to watch her. She goes across the street and chooses a thin birch. She plants her feet in front of the tree, then squats, staring at her knees. I wonder if I'm becoming weird.

She stands again, tugging down the hem of her skirt. She doesn't even look when she steps onto the highway. She stands there in the middle of the asphalt. She lifts up one heel, wiping off the mud with toilet paper. Then she does the same to the other heel.

When she slides back into the seat, one of the babushkas holds out the paper hat of sunflower seeds to her and says, "Here, girl, you need to eat."

"There's no place to wash hands," Choika says.

The police come aboard, forcing their way to the back of the bus. They crowbar the locked bathroom door open and a tower of shoeboxes collapses on them. The driver breaks for it, but Andre and Vadim trounce him in the aisle.

"You bitches," the driver says. "They were in on it," he says to the police as they bend him over the seatback and cuff him. "They wanted free pairs. Size forty-three and forty-five. Check them."

"A cunt to your mouth," someone in back yells. "You unscrupulous shit-ass," another.

Choika stands awkwardly, like she has to sneeze, and whips some kind of ball with wires out of her bag. She pushes something on it and hunches. She hunches again, like she's pushing in the top of a deflated volleyball with her thumbs.

"What is this?" one of the babushkas says.

I close my eyes.

When I open them again the aisle is a knot of perfectly unharmed screaming bodies.

"Move," Andre says to me and I push out into the aisle.

The soldiers lunge across the seat, tackling Choika. A policeman pitches the bomb out the window. It lands in the street and rolls into the ditch.

As I'm swept off the bus, I'm thinking, Did she have that bomb before I thought it? "Did I do that?" I say out loud, and in English, but no one can hear me.

Once off the bus the soldiers yell furiously for us to get as far away from the bomb as possible. We are off the bus, dispersing into the woods, I more hesitantly than the group.

When the police stuff Choika into the back of the cop car I can see her knees are bleeding but she's not crying or shaking. She sits in the backseat staring out the window just like she'd stared out the bus window the whole ride, like nothing mattered.

The police and the soldiers crouch over the bomb. Andre tinkers with it and Vadim and the police back up.

"I never saw a Muslim dressed like that," one of the babushkas says.

"She was masquerading as one of our girls," the other says. "Sluts," she says and dumps a little purse full of coins on the ground.

"What are you doing?" one babushka says.

"She gave me four rubles for the toilet paper."

A little boy runs up and starts collecting the money. His mother yells at him to put it down and come back to her. When he does she hugs his head and says, "I wish we'd be there" or something like that—I don't understand the exact phrasing.

I approach the soldiers and the police. Andre is still fiddling with the bomb.

"I know her name," I say.

The police turn around. Their faces twitch. They're really shaken up. "Who are you?" one of them asks.

"Foreigner," Vadim says.

"I know her name," I say. "I heard her say it."

"It's crap," Andre says, "total crap." He leaves the bomb in the ditch. "What's her name?" Andre says.

"Choika," I say.

"Choika," one of the police says. He says it again louder and looking her way and she turns her head. I suddenly feel ashamed, like I gave her up.

"What is that?" Andre says. "Choika."

"Chukchi?" Vadim says.

"Never heard of it," Andre says.

"Friends," the driver says. He's still in the handcuffs. "Feel free to retake your seat, friend," the driver says to me.

I'm the first one back on the bus and one of Choika's gorgeous shoes is on the floor near my seat. There's a scrap of toilet paper stuck to the bottom of the heel.

The driver talks to the police and the soldiers as the other passengers reboard, absolutely silent. Even the chatty babushkas. They sit cramped together in the exact same spots they sat in before, leaving a wide space where Choika had been. A policeman unlocks the driver's handcuffs and he comes aboard. He goes back to the bathroom and selects two boxes, restacking those that had fallen. The door refuses to latch at first but eventually clicks. He hands the two boxes to the policemen. Then the soldiers and the driver reboard.

I point to the shoe on the ground.

"Don't touch it," Andre says. "Forget about it." He kicks

it under the seat and hands me a beer. From the first sip, I feel the pressure build in my bladder.

The driver stands at the front of the bus. "Any more crazy terrorists here?" he says. No one says anything. "I sure hope not. Next stop is Novgorod. Unfortunately, I'm sorry to say, that the bathroom on the bus is still out of order."

Our Cause

I KNEW WE WERE IN FOR TROUBLE THE MOMENT the locals, who call resort workers "spank tourists," showed. Suddenly, from out of nowhere, a crowd of Carhartt flannels. We couldn't figure who invited them. It was me and Patsy and a few others who have jobs like vacuuming moose heads in the main lodge.

I tried to make them feel welcome. Patsy was the only woman and loving it. I offered them some detergent. We did bumps in the bathroom in case management descended. We got off-kilter and imprecise, and the detergent flew, dusting the floor and toilet seat.

Then I taught them all how to dryer-ride. I programmed thirty-second spins in the Vapor Electro-Heat Roller Dryer, which beat them up good. I gave instruction and advice: Roll at precisely nine o'clock. Land frog push-ups.

All the while I kept my arm locked around Patsy's, knowing how she gets with men like this around. At one point she broke away, saying that she had to go to toilet. She always says this: *go to toilet.* I don't know where the *the* goes.

About then the locals suggested that it was my turn in the dryer, that I should show them how it's done. I said, "Nah, fellas. I get into this all the time. It's you all's moment." Brick, the biggest one, put his hand on my shoulder and said, "Really, I would like to see what you can do."

You do not go this far, all of the locals dizzy and warm to the touch, without taking your fair shake. I glanced around and noted that all the moose head vacuumers had left already. It was just me, Patsy, and the Carhartt flannels. I climbed in and at that moment Patsy returned from the bathroom. She wore the feather roach clip in her hair. She switched on the boom box and I heard muffled new wave country reverberating through the dryer drum. I remembered her telling me at the start of the trip, "One thing you've got to realize, Scoma, I am the type of girl who eats her pudding with a fork." She was skeptical about how a winter spent washing rich people's come out of sheets was going to fix us.

Brick hooked his arm around her elbow and spun her into the open floor. One of the other locals tapped on the dryer control pad, and I could tell from the three beeps he didn't program me the same thirty-second joyride I programmed them.

I had a perfect view of Brick and Patsy out of the dryer glass, and I simply employed my technique, turned at nine o'clock, landed frog push-ups. Simple. Just like I told them it'd be. They applauded for me. Patsy gyrated on Brick's leg. Brick spun his arm above his head like a lasso. It's nothing I hadn't seen before, used to recline with a BLT while she wiggled it on some creampuff's haunch.

I dryer-ride these days better than I skate vert. But when I saw the whole group of them through the glass, her and the locals heading out of what we might call the public area of the facility and into the back, I mistimed and came down hard. The metal drum knobs slamboed me. I got caught in the revolutions and couldn't get out. I could feel the blood racing to the contours of every future bruise.

Patsy danced her way out of what we might call the public area of the facility, finger-tip-feeling the underside of Brick's chin, not her slinky stripper dance but kind of Indiana, slithering ledges. She walked them right out there with those ledges, one of which Brick tried to tame. She fired it at him.

They didn't take her. She left with them.

Everyone told me. "Damn, Scoma," they said, "that girl lives in a necklace." I thought that if I could get her away from the place where she shed her clothes while folks mowed the breakfast buffet, we'd be all right.

When the dryer cycle stopped, I pushed the door open and flopped out. I lay on the floor and the wooden trusses cutting across the middle of the ceiling spun like helicopter blades for a long time. When they finally slowed, I stumbled to the back. The locals were all passed out in the dirty sheets, our neglected responsibility. Wrapped together tightly in sheets, Brick and Patsy.

I toppled one of the laundry carts for commotion.

Brick's eyes popped open. He tried to roll away from Patsy but he was tangled in the sheets. I punched his face a few times before he got up. Patsy didn't wake. She lay there nude, curled on her side like a letter S. And he was facing me, fists up.

Now, I took some boxing. I threw a few jabs, missed. He ducked, bobbed. His dick and balls smacked around, distracting me. He didn't even try to cover himself. I remembered hearing somewhere that naked men don't fight good.

The trickle of blood from his nose got me

overconfident, and I threw a knockout, a real Popeye. I missed again, over extended, still dizzy. I have this habit of sticking my tongue out during physical activity. He got underneath me with the uppercut, a nice one.

What I remember last is the tip of my tongue sailing away from me.

When I come to, there's a tarantula in my mouth. My knee is wedged under the emergency brake. A ziplock baggie on Patsy's feather roach clip dangles from the rearview mirror. Inside the baggie is some kind of salted slug.

There are no operative mirrors in the Civvie. Ditches snapped off the side-views. At first I think I might have been in a wreck. Then it all comes roaring back to me. Not a tarantula, the swollen nub—what's left of my tongue. That would make the salted slug the unfortunate tip. The rearview mirror is stuck in that mode where headlights don't shine in your eyes and all you can see is a transparent reflection of yourself.

I un-wedge my knee from the emergency brake. I squeeze the tip of my tongue in the ziplock baggie. Me and Patsy drove to Big Sky Resort from Florida just a few weeks ago to spend our winter working laundry. Right about now, on an ordinary morning, we would have already laundered the very sheets her and Brick are probably still twisted up in. We'd be pushing them in carts up to the resort. We'd have folded tight and flat. We'd have tucked in corners to boomerang them at maids and run.

I don't go back inside the laundry room to get her or ask how it was I am put into the Civvie. I drive away. I drive until I see a Taco Bell and utilize the facilities. I wad up a ball of toilet paper and press it to the swollen nub of my tongue.

Flecks of toilet paper stick to it. I self-serve a cup of ice, pushing the tip of my tongue—ziplock baggie, roach clip, and all—down in there. The boy at the checkout eyes my blood-smeared face and hand. He doesn't say anything. Then I drive away from Montana. I'm all giddy, delirious, lightheaded. I am going ninety, minus some percentage of tongue.

The road in front of me is blank, interrupted every couple miles with dead deer. I start to count out loud like Patsy and I always did, and that brings on the tears. I punch the steering wheel. Sixteen, seventeen, seventeen and a half, eighteen—how much for torso? Leg? A furry stain? How do you count that? Me and Patsy tried. We counted carcasses in high fractions, her always looking way over the ditch, singing, "Four and two-twenty-eights. Where's the hell the rest of the thing go?"

Right before the state border, there's a line of trucks parked on the shoulder. I slow to a crawl and roll down the window. A bumper sticker on a Chevy reads, "Gut Deer?" There's a huddle of folks with knives and Igloo coolers in the ditch. They're knelt around a moose carcass in the snow.

A pear-shaped guy with ice in his beard waves at me. He is holding a lime-green paring knife. When he comes toward me I see the moose's side is split open. I've never seen a dead thing so big. Maybe a thousand pounds. There's a chain between the Gut Deer? truck's hitch and the moose's leg. A trail marks where the chain dragged the moose from the road. Another guy buries the guts in the snow a few feet away. Steam rises when he shovels snow over the guts.

"You signed up?" the guy says. A Ford Pinto honks and screams around me. I make my face into a question. "Buzzard Workshop," the guy says. "Roadkill 101. You signed up?" His tone is recruity. I figure, it's a curious scene. I figure, I'll check it out. I pull the car over.

"You got a blade?" he asks. I point to my mouth and shake my head. "It's okay," he says. "We have some spares."

He opens the door to the Gut Deer? truck and hands me a hunting knife with a compass in the butt of the handle, the flea market kind I used to covet as a kid. Then we walk to the moose carcass and the old lady and a woman with a green bandana tied around her head scoot aside to make room for me. I kneel next to the moose's shoulder.

There's a girl about my age wearing a Skoal T-shirt that matches the guy shoveling guts into the snow and a woman sitting in a lawn chair behind the moose reading a copy of *Better Homes & Gardens*. The bearded guy stands at the moose's head. The smell is warm and sour.

The bearded guy hands out oversized freezer bags, then props his boot on one of its antlers and begins to lecture: "Now as I was saying, roadkill is a right and a privilege…" He says some things I don't understand about anatomy and about the unjust laws we are in violation of by taking apart this already-murdered creature in the ditch. I want to clarify. It does not seem right that something like this would be illegal. But I can't speak. My tongue swells, filling my mouth.

Then the moose's carcass vibrates, and I realize everyone is cutting into it. The bearded guy appears behind me. He takes my hand, which is holding the hunting knife, and guides me through the muscle of the shoulder. It's thick, tougher than I ever imagined. Once the knife is in, he releases me and traces the line in front of the knife with his finger as I work it—the meat pushing against the blade before opening a seam. I manage around what you might call a hock.

"That'a boy," he says and pats my shoulder. An old lady crouched over the moose holds up something red and stringy in her veined hands.

"Can you eat this?" she shouts to the bearded guy.

"Leave something for the real buzzards," he says. They laugh.

He moves on to the woman in the bandana whose knife is stuck in some dense material around the back leg. I'm wearing thin black gloves and my hands start to go numb from the cold. I split my hock into two freezer bags. When I look up, the woman in the bandana is smiling and cradling the detached leg. She says that she used to butcher moose she found on the road with a chainsaw. She is thankful for this clean cut. She is thankful for the bearded guy sharing his expertise with us like this. "Being able to take an entire leg off," the old woman says, "to know how to work the knife and find the joints."

She is taking both back legs, for living-room lamps, she says. She stands them up against an Igloo cooler. The other two are rationed out for soup bone and marrow. The girl in the Skoal T-shirt slices off the tail, about the size of a yam, and slips it into her coat pocket.

The bearded guy pries open the moose's mouth, revealing its tongue, which is like a giant purple snail. "Who wants to pickle this beauty?" he asks, sawing at the back of the tongue with the thin paring knife. It ekes out like a monstrous conch. He holds it in his gloved hand and it seems to pulse. I bolt to the Civvie, abandoning the freezer bags and my hock. "Hey," the bearded guy yells. I drive away and only realize that I stole his knife when I look down and see it bloodying my passenger seat.

I tear into Wyoming on a little route. And when a prairie dog farm with a little store is the first thing that appears, I make it my first Wyoming thing.

A sign says *Dawg Food Here* and the bells on the door rattle me. I see aquariums imprisoning wimpy rattlesnakes, and underneath the aquariums are bags of peanuts costing one dollar, prairie dog food. But *I'm* hungry for nuts, and go for one. When I take it, a shriveled rattler strikes the glass.

I say, "mirror" to the old man behind the counter but it comes out "*mewe*" and a spot of blood on his collar. He points toward the back of the store, where there's a bathroom and another sign, *If you find this bathroom a mess PLEASE tell us*. The bathroom is stunningly clean—the mirror, though old, recently Windexed.

I stick out the nub of my tongue. I rinse with water, then pop a peanut and the salt wakes up whatever's dying in there. I rub at the red stains around my lips. The stains fade but don't come off.

On my way out, stringy old dude asks, "Is the bathroom clean enough?" I thumbs-up and leave. Then I am outside on a corralled field. A hanging wooden sign reads, *Little D Guest Ranch*. The dogs pop out. I sprinkle some peanuts in the snow at my feet. They mob, chittering like a flock of pigeons.

There's a yellow Kelty tent—a nice one—over in the corner and someone pops out in the same way the dogs just did. He is bound in skintight Gore-Tex head to toe, arctic gear, the kind that the rich resort people wear to look like ninjas while they ski. He walks toward me, all knees, and puts his hands on his hips.

Suddenly I'm overcome by tired. I try some signing: point at his tent, then put my palms together like prayer and tilt my head onto them.

"Temp arrangement," he says. "I'm here on business. The old man doesn't mind. He's senile on clean. And sure it's abnatural domestication but you won't gain anything by setting them free. They've got a good thing here, to them. And what the fuck do they know? We're the ones who are supposed to know things."

I empty the last of the nuts in the snow and the dogs feeding frenzy. I pull out my chest and the Marlboro tent. I've been going around with the chest since I was ten. I keep it in the trunk of the Civvie at all times for precisely a chain of circumstances like this: my escape from an already cold and treacherous environs populated with wealthy skiing ninjas to one colder and more treacherous and populated with small rodents.

"I've got a good thing here," the guy says. "What can you offer in exchange for my letting you share this space?" I set the chest in the snow. I walk around to the passenger side and take the hunting knife. I stick it into the snow to wet it and wipe the blade on my pants. I hand it to him handle-end first. He takes, breathes heavy on it and wipes it again on his Gore-Tex, looks at his reflection in it. "Okay," he says. "Good. You're good."

I carry the chest and Marlboro tent across the farm. The snow is slushy here. I imagine it's the heat emitted by all the creature bodies below the surface. Their holes are clear and visible in the snow. The dogs pop up and chirp at me. I spit blood at them and they disappear again. I stake at the other end of the farm from the yellow Kelty, find a spot between holes big enough for the Marlboro tent.

"Let me tell you something," the guy shouts across the farm. "Prairie dogs have a more than 300-utterance vocabulary to identify predators alone. We're not dealing with dumb animals here. So show some respect or I'll have to knife you. We're in their space."

I unload the contents of my chest on the floor of the tent for insulation. There's a checklist taped to the inside lid. It's from my summer camp, a slightly modified list of the camp's recommendations on what kids should keep with them. Nowadays I'm good with a slingshot, I know how to bust up dogfights, I rile like a motherfucker, but still hold to it:

wash cloths 2	flashlight 1	underpants 8
slingshot 1	T-shirts 12	PJ boxers 3
pillows 1	flannel shirt 1	sleep shirt 1
pillow cases 2	~~collar shirts 2~~	flip-flops 1
sheets 4	camo shirt/pants 1	water hose 1
slingshot ammo 2 packs	shorts 8	high-tops 2
blanket (brown) 1	Marlboro tent 1	cords 1
sleeping bag 1	rain poncho 1	jerky sticks 2
laundry bag 1	socks 8	skateboard 1

I climb into my PJ boxers and the sleeping bag. I snack some jerky, which burns what's left of my tongue, and roll around on my bruises through the night, occasionally waking to watch my breath hanging in the air.

Next the guy is clanging a pair of trowels outside the tent-flap, and it is morning. "Chores," he says. I step outside and he looks at me like he expects me to say something. I point to my mouth and stick out the nub of my tongue. Then he walks a line in the snow—wide, deliberate steps—bifurcating His Side from My Side. He gives me a little more, but I accept since I'm the rookie. "It's their home," he says. "The least we can do is dig them out." I notice a thin layer of snow has fallen overnight. I watch what he does as he walks around the farm, tapping his foot in front of him until he finds a prairie dog hole. Then he kneels down and carves out all the snow with the trowel. As he goes, the dogs pop out behind him, looking calm and reassured. I turn to my own tent, the top of which is sagging slightly under an inch of snow.

"Things don't even know to hibernate anymore," he says. "They come out in this freezing fuck cold weather 'cause someone presents them a high-fructose trans-fattening cookie."

I follow his lead and dig out some holes. Most of the snow falls into the hole when I stick the trowel through, and I wonder if we're doing them much of a favor at all. When we're done he waves me over to his Kelty.

"These are my things," he says, unzipping the Kelty and pointing to a neat arrangement of objects across the floor of the tent. "Don't you get any ideas." He opens a shoebox and sifts through some vials.

He possesses the following items:

-a one-person yellow Kelty pup tent shaped like a cocoon
-shoebox full of vials
-a Toshiba laptop with cellular modem
-two trowels
-a fish-shaped wooden cutting board
-the bearded guy's hunting knife

He selects a vial then looks back at me, changes his mind and takes another. He turns the vial over in his palm, and there are ten or so white pellets, half the size of BBs rolling around there.

"For your mouth problem," he says. "Take it." It's so much easier to do what he says than to try arguing without words. I touch my tongue to one and it's straight sugar. The sweet stings worse than salt. I tip my head back and the pellets dissolve all over my throat. He gives me the vial. "Repeat three times a day."

Then a Westfalia stops on the little route and beeps. He zips up his Kelty, gets in the Westfalia, and leaves.

I say, "*mewe*" again to stringy old dude. "Yes, son," he says. "Yes, go on." Then he comes over the counter. "You know what, son," he says, "accompany me." I follow him into the bathroom and he swivels the plastic grommets holding the mirror to the wall. "You know what, take the mirror. Take it."

I take it. I hold it out and look at myself. It's a good mirror, thick, heavy, a little magnification. The reflection is rubbed off some at the edges. I can see the black follicles on the outside of my nose and the crusted blood in the cracks of my lips.

"It's too dirty for me. Impossible to clean. I don't even want to look at myself in it."

"*Unks*," I say.

"You're welcome, son," he says. "Welcome to you."

I take the mirror back to the Marlboro tent and prop it against the chest. I refill the Taco Bell cup with snow and cram in the ziplock baggie and the tip of my tongue. Then I watch myself, but all I can see is that image of Brick and Patsy curled up in the sheets. I clip Patsy's feather roach clip to my ear and it pinches. When I get sick of pinching my ear, I sit in the open tent-flap. Cars pull up and little kids bundled up like croissants flick peanuts at the dogs. Sometimes the kids point at me. The dads put hands on the kids' heads and lead them back to their cars. For a long time I watch people before I start feeling queasy and crawl back into the sleeping bag.

I get the sensation I am sleeping on a decline, like I'm slipping, but I know the ground's perfectly flat here. Plains. I walk outside and around the tent to make sure, then lie back down and the slipping starts again. I get these moments of panic, when I slide and jerk. This goes on for hours. I feel dizzy and tired, but when I close my eyes, a few seconds go by and I jolt awake, dizzy and tired again.

Later, I leave the prairie dog farm, walk as far as I can see into the distance, hop barbed wires. The flat state goes on and on, covered in a thin layer of snow. I remember that resort trainer's pitch our first day at Big Sky. "Welcome to Montana and sustainable employ under the biggest sky in the continental fifty." Me and Patsy were impressed by this, that we were working under the biggest sky. Standing here though, you can see how at the edges the Earth curves. *This* is bigger sky.

On the way back, some wind gusts swell up and something blows into my eye. At first I think it's just snow, but when I blink it all out, there's this black speck at the corner of my vision. I try to rub it off my face but can't seem to find the speck with my finger. Back at the tent, I check it in my mirror, and there's nothing other than my wet red face.

Then I realize the dot I'm looking at is not exactly on my face but between the edge of my peripheral and the top of my cheek, hovering there. I check the mirror again. Nothing on the eye or my face. Impossible, I think. Maybe it's on my eye. But if it were on my eye it would move as my eye moved.

I sniff the sugar pills. Then I lie down and I don't slip or slide or jolt awake.

Later, I sense a presence and poke my head out. It is dark already. One of the dogs has opened a burrow at the door to my tent and a perturbed sneeze echoes from down there. The guy pecks at his Toshiba by a fire in front of the Kelty.

I join him, sit on a log by the fire. His tent has a flap that comes out and covers us and the log. It's comforting to sit under a flap. I unsheathe a jerky for myself. He glares.

"It doesn't bother you that creature's guts were killed for your consumption?" he says.

I shake my head no. Then I gesture for the computer. He hands it to me. On screen he's still logged into a chat room called Loggerheads, where he's typed, *I'm talking anvil-educating teat, pinhead.* He scoots beside me so he can read as I type.

I like animals, I type. *I just don't see the problem with eating them.*

"What's your cause then?" he asks. "Me? Recovering eco-terrorist." With the hunting knife, he shaves a hair off the part of his arm showing between his glove and the sleeve of his coat.

My motto is 'Pave Earth.'

"That's not a cause," he says. "Posture maybe, at best."

I type, *I'm seeing a black spot orbit of my cheekbone. This afternoon I thought I was falling while I was asleep. What do you have me on?*

He checks me out. Moves his head all around my face. "Point to the black spot," he says, blinking. I have to turn to the fire to locate it in the dark. I put my finger to where it appears in the glow on my fingernail.

"That's not unexpected really. Our bodies are in a trepidatious state of balance," he says. He says there's something wrong inside of me, that an ordinary doctor would treat the symptoms, doing me no good, and that his stuff is going after the problem. "There's bound to be some misfires as it works out your real malfunction." He pops into his tent and returns with a new vial of sugar pills. "Take the exact same amount of these as you did the other ones." He pauses, then says, "Except double. It means you're getting better."

I type, *No symptom. Problem is I bit off the tip of my tongue.*

"Don't kid yourself. You wouldn't have bit your tongue off if there wasn't already an imbalance somewhere. That you did it was a symptom. Never treat the symptom. It only encourages it."

He takes the Toshiba back and tells me his name is Minnow. He tells me as a kid he ran away from charges of plunking firecrackers into gas tanks. He ran to an Indian reservation somewhere in California. There was a marsh on the reservation, which he slipped into when the cops showed. It was filled with minnows, Minnow says. The Indians didn't really hide him, but they didn't give him up either. They walked the police around the whole reservation, including the marsh. The minnows nibbled at his ears the whole time, he says. When the police left, he came out and the Indians anointed him Minnow. They allowed him to live with them for the next few years because they admired how long he could hold his breath.

"That was the start of it all," he says. "Me and those slim fish hovering under the water together, hiding out." I reach for the laptop, but he donks my hand with the compass on the hunting knife. "Don't talk," he says. "Listen."

He tells me that he spent the day picketing a housing development in the forests just northwest. He says one year ago he'd have napalmed the whole block, but now he chants and holds hands with other protestors.

"I'm getting better too," he says.

The dogs are more active at night. We can't see them but they paw in the snow around us.

"Watch this," he says. He touches his throat and a sound, a cross between turkey gobble and suction cup, comes out. The dogs scramble for their holes. He laughs and says, "P-dog for *owl*."

I try and remember that sound, but I find the image of Brick and Patsy in my head again and by the time I've remembered what it was I was trying to remember, I've forgotten the sound. Then I silently vow to myself never to do any of the things Patsy and I used to do together ever again. Like counting the deer carcasses on the highway as I drive. And like laundry. I vow to never do laundry again. It reminds me too much of her. I convert that vow into a silent prayer. I spend the whole night thinking, "God, please help me to do no more laundry, ever again. I know there is that thing about cleanliness next to godliness, but it will give me great pain to wash clothes, because I feel I can never do that without thinking of her."

Back in my Marlboro tent, I admire Minnow because he stands for something. Except for Patsy, I stand for nothing. I have no cause. So mine must be to forget her. I drift to sleep watching that black speck hovering like a defector beauty mark.

When the speck disappears and my left elbow sprouts a wart, I throw away my dirty sleep shirt. Minnow gives me sugar pills from a new vial. I keep the Taco Bell cup packed with snow. The tip of my tongue and roach clip are frozen in there. When the wart disappears and spider veins emerge along my left thigh, I plug up a high-traffic burrow near my tent-flap with the PJ boxers I've been wearing for a month. Minnow changes the sugar pill prescription again. When the spider veins fade away, a patch of leg hair falls out on my right calf and the bald spot tingles for a week. Minnow explains that he is chasing down my real problem, and he's almost got it.

The leg hair returns—what looks like sprinkles of pepper on my calf. And after, as it sprouts into hair, nothing happens for a few days. Then the strangest thing, I wake up one night to a scratching at the tent-flap. The wind is wilder than usual but the snow is beginning to melt, signaling the beginning of the end of the resort season. I unzip the tent-flap and see the *Dawg Food Here* sign tumbleweeding across the snowy plain in the wind. A chirp makes me look down and there is a dog halfway out of the burrow. I'd swear it's the exact burrow that I plugged up with the PJ boxers, and I wonder if it ate them or maybe used them for bedding.

"Your tongue will grow back," it says in a squeaky voice. "You may think it's something magical, but it's not. It's basically just skin. Meat and skin, and it will grow back. It will heal, not unlike a wound, and then you will go find me—I mean her. Give me a jerky stick."

It's looking at me. I recognize her by her grey eyes.

"Okay, so you've found me out," the prairie dog says. "I was never good with deception. Never even bothered with it. I'm sorry about the thing with the local. He was a big man and sometimes big men woo me."

I hold out a jerky. The prairie dog snatches it with its teeth.

I want to ask it if it's a hallucination. And how is it halfway out of the burrow? Is it levitating there? Or does the burrow curve such that it can stand like that? I say, "Are you a symptom?" and it replies, "Please." I toss another jerky and eat one myself. I sit there with the tent-flap open watching the prairie dog, and the prairie dog sits there half out of the hole blinking back at me.

When it finishes the second jerky, it disappears down its burrow and I zip up the tent-flap.

In the morning, like every morning, I stick out my tongue at the mirror. I see something new and open the tent-flap to let more light in. Tiny buds all along the severed edge, small pinkish buds and buds on top of buds on top of buds, mini-cauliflower clusters—regrowth.

Minnow tosses a trowel through the tent-flap. I stick out my tongue and emerge pointing at my face, but he doesn't pay attention. "There's an emergency, Scoma. Hurry." He's ignoring His Side or My Side. He's running and digging out burrows. I'm slower, feeling hung-over though I haven't drank since Montana.

I trowel a hole and a dog pops out, spooking me. The prairie dog makes a laugh sound and disappears again.

"*Bitssss*," I say.

"I need a big favor, Scoma," he says. "A chicken farm was wrecked by freak winter tornados last night. Now they're going to slaughter them. If you can drive, we can run some recon."

There is no question I owe him. I go to the chest for my camo shirt/pants set and we drive with the sheet flapping behind the Civvie like a cape.

"Did you hear what they're calling you?" Minnow says.

I turn my mouth into an "o" and pinch my eyebrows together.

"The dogs," he says. "You're Feh-feh. "

"*Veh-veh?*" I say.

"You should be flattered. Technically, that's not a predator name. They understand, you and me are with them."

He flips on the radio news and it gives us the whole story. Inexplicable tornados. Took out a chicken farm on the edge of the state. Sixty-four laying-hen buildings, each 600 feet long and 50 feet wide, 85,000 chickens per. Inoperable watering, feeding, and heating systems. They say they can't be saved. It's too dangerous. So, more than one million chickens will be killed to prevent them from dying. An interview with some Department of Agriculture poser: "Under state law, they need to be buried or burned or rendered. And the process has to be done humanely too. These chickens are not going to die of cold."

"God damn right-on about that," Minnow says. He begins shaking. "When we get there my people will have certain—how should we say?—oh fuck it. If someone tells you to do something, do it. And don't follow me. I hate that."

I look away when we pass road kill. And there is nothing else but that big wide sky and then a city of warehouse-like things appear in the distance and the traffic bottlenecks. The laying houses are arranged in six perfectly symmetrical rows. The tornadoes have lifted the roofs off several and the smell of bird shit is heavy in the air. We slow to a crawl. Finally, cars pull over and we do too and walk toward the chicken farm. I recognize the heat of the breath of many small, nervous creatures.

We walk the line of stickered cars. There's tree, bird, and Operation Ivy stickers, X's, little fig leaves, a bumper that reads ANABAPTIST AND PROUD OF IT. And then there's all the government issue, the emergency vehicles, a snorkel truck. I misdetect at first, but folks peel out of the way for us. Pretty soon the street is packed with punks and hippies and funny hats all whipping around, then making way. It looks more like the run-up to a Lollapalooza than a chicken protest, and Minnow is the Perry Farrel. He swaggers, an "I'm in charge here" on the tip of his tongue, more and more buds on mine.

When we hit the perimeter, the Agriculture Spokesman, surrounded by firemen, is giving a speech: "There's nothing to be done for them. We've saved all we can. The new plan is to gas the laying houses, then render. We'll need you folks to disband."

"We'll all carry out one," Minnow says. "One man, one bird!"

The crowd chants, "One man, one bird. One bird, one man." Someone in back shouts, "One woman."

"The buildings are a tangle of cages and chickens and manure pits below. This is going to be a Herculean task," the spokesman says.

"You don't need a Hercules to carry one chicken," Minnow cries.

"Don't need a Hercules to carry one chicken," the crowd chants. "One man, one bird."

"Woman," the voice in back shouts again, drowned out in the second chorus of "Hercules."

"The danger is too great to allow people inside the buildings to, as much as we'd like, rescue the birds," the spokesman says.

Minnow backs into the crowd, chanting and punching fists into the air at the spokesman. I don't follow him. I walk down the road a bit to the point where the crowd thins and sit on a snow-covered rock, wetting my camo pants. I stare at the dismantled laying houses. I can make out the off-white puffs that are the chickens, pacing in their cages. I hear the low rumble of a mass clucking.

I roll my eyes, checking for the long gone defector beauty mark, and touch my finger to the multiplying bumps on my tongue. Then I feel a shove on my shoulder and turn to see the pear-shaped bearded guy from the Buzzard Workshop. I stand up. "You're the one run off with my knife," he says. He towers over me.

"*Canth theak*," I say.

He stares.

I point to my mouth.

"Where's my knife?"

I pat my pockets, and hold out my empty palms.

"I've run into your type before," he says. "Only just they never stole my knife. Every year hundreds of moose are killed by cars or trains. Hundreds. A road-killed moose is a unique opportunity. One hundred and twenty-five pounds of meat will stock a freezer for a year. That's just over 25 percent of a moose. It's not like deer. Deer you hang to sweeten the meat. You can taste the difference between a back strap and a brisquet. Moose is different altogether. It's a community event. It's environmentally sound. It's a lot of fun."

I nod and shrug, hoping he'll understand, I didn't run away to antagonize his cause. I didn't mean to steal the knife. A body alone is not capable of communicating this.

"I don't know about your type," the bearded guy says. He turns and I watch him climb into his Gut Deer? truck.

From the opposite direction, gas trucks break the long horizon. The crowd has begun to peel out, to admit defeat. The drivers of the gas trucks receive some instructions from the Agriculture Spokesman, and they park in front of a laying house. They run hoses inside the buildings and pull massive plastic tarps over them one by one.

I'm getting cold. The orange sun is setting. Plus, I realize that I really don't want to be here when all these chickens die.

Then I see what seems to me to be two skiers from the resort, in their ninja gear, something—maybe skis—between them. Then it crystallizes, it's Minnow and someone else and the thing they're wielding may be a giant can opener. I try and block the reflection of the sun off the snow with my hand.

"They've got the Jaws of Life," someone screams. Two firemen bolt down the embankment. The clunky fire suits make their legs short, and they run stilted.

Minnow and his co-conspirator rake the Jaws of Life across the bottom edge of the cages along an exposed section of the laying house. The gas truck drivers drop their tarps and converge on them. One of the firemen trips and goes face first into the snow, his yellow fire helmet like something obscene but natural growing in the winter. Before I know it, I too am running down the embankment toward them.

Minnow and the other guy are prying up the cut edge of the cage, opening one whole side of the enclosure, releasing what might be thousands of them simultaneously.

"Go," Minnow screams.

One of the firemen tackles him and the gas truck guys go for his friend, but they're slowed stepping through all the bewildered chickens. The sound, that rumble of clucking, is off the charts when I reach them.

The chickens hop and flutter. White feathers hang in the air, but at first I think it's snowing again. Everywhere you step is bird. The snow comes up to their bellies and they fumble, moving like popping corn across the field.

The fireman is holding Minnow's hands behind his back. He's face first in the snow. He looks up and I see that he is bawling. He is biting his upper lip, gazing out across the snow— between here and the horizon there is nothing but the remains of the laying house roofs and a spreading band of chickens clearing the perimeter into only deeper snow.

Minnow sees me and mouths, "Go." I glance to my left and see the other fireman, up now and beelining for me. I run behind the birds shouting at them to go, go, go, go, go. I snatch one up and it's warm in my hands. I tuck it under my arm like a football. I pick a point where the snow meets the big sky, and I aim to make it there.

The Taste of Penny

BROTHERMAN'S HAS A LITTLE PROBLEM WITH ITS local competitors, The Two Men And A Truck crew. The Two Men And A Truck crew are former cops.

Now Sam is standing on the side of the road with a current cop, and his finger, a part of himself which he loathes, pokes into the meaty ball in the corner of his eye. At first he's shocked to see the thing there and thinks it's someone else's. But he recognizes the sad condition of his own digit in the bright glare of the street light as it misses his nose completely.

This sad condition was a constant source of embarrassment. Just the other day two girls, strangers in some waiting area, suggested that he get a manicure.

"I don't even know you," he said to them.

"They're really bad," one of them said, "your nails."

"But do you think it's your place to tell someone something like that?"

"They're disgusting," said the other one.

Sam had always known they were disgusting fingers, spindly and crooked from breaking them as a kid. He couldn't recall ever having a full nail. He bit them down to nothing—a habit he'd recently been trying to break, going around with hot sauce coating them, reeking of cayenne and vinegar.

The surprise of that one appearing where it isn't supposed to and sticking him in the eye makes him lose track of the penny hidden under his tongue, and swallow it.

Immediately Sam begins—maybe this isn't the right word—*sensing* the penny in his stomach. He experiences two distinct sensations: the pressure of his palm on the back of his eyelid, and the discomfort of the penny inside him, a presence. If he moves the hand, pain lights up in his eye.

Sam and the cop stand there a few silent minutes looking at each other on the side of the road. The cop looks at Sam, and Sam looks at the cop. Sam blinks his good eye. He keeps the other eye covered with his palm, pointing his fingers outward like lashes. He doesn't even want to touch himself with them. Not in the eye, not on his dick. He wants to keep his fingers away from himself.

Sam doesn't know what to do with his other arm so it hangs limp at his side. He does not have his swerve on.

"So it's like that is it?" the cop says.

"Like how?"

There is no response.

"I think I really did something to my eye," Sam says. "I can't seem to take my hand away from it."

"You know what I think, sir?" the cop says.

"I don't know."

"I'll tell you. I think your eye's not hurt. I think you're

trying to get out of something." The cop believes Sam to be bullshitting. He believes him to be drunk as well.

"Oh it's hurt. It's definitely hurt."

"And I don't suppose you could pass any more tests then, huh?"

"It'd be difficult. I am happy to try. It'd not be easy. Not one bit. However I am cooperative. I will do what you ask. I am being cooperative."

The cop walks Sam to the squad car. He jostles him some, testing his swerve for himself. Sam is steadfast. Never mind he missed his nose. Sam is the best drunk driver you'll meet. He'd been pulled over not because of the seatbelt either. No one can see that you're not wearing your seatbelt. Everyone knows that is some bullshit excuse law. He'd been pulled for his magnetic signs, and he should have known better.

He'd won them off a sign painter, in a drinking contest, and he could peel them off at any time. But they were fantastic white magnetic signs, and Sam was proud of them. They announced in the way the constant flyering at the grocery store didn't that he ran a real business. In beveled yellow letters, a yellow so fantastic you could almost call it neon, "Brotherman's Hauling."

But this is only Sam's perspective. Actually he is a piss-poor drunk driver. He has been for years.

"Remove your mitt from your facial area." Sam does and brushes the cop's cheek. "Jesus Christ," the cop says. "Watch those things."

"Apology," Sam says.

"Now open it."

Sam tries, but he can only manage a tight squint. Everything is blurred, and the effort it takes to open that one forces the other one closed.

"How many fingers am I holding?" the cop says.

"I have no idea." Which he does not. He sees refracted light, lots of refracted light, and shapes.

"Well don't lay down back there," the cop says.

"Why would I lay down?"

"Some people lay down." The cop shuts the door behind him then climbs in the front and radios for an ambulance. With the dispatcher, he refers to Sam as "some numb nuts who seems to have poked his own eye during the drunk test."

Sam instinctively begins to gnaw on the thumbnail of his spare hand. He need not even, as he usually does, remind himself of the protein in fingernail.

When the cop opens the door again, he has a little gadget with a tube coming off it. "While we're waiting, you don't need neither one of your eyes to blow into this."

There'd been no problem when the Two Men stuck to moving. But maybe the moving business wasn't too hot or something. Just last week they stumbled across a flyer at the PriceChopper that read, "Two Men And A Truck: Moving, AND NOW HAULING TOO." Technically, yes, movers and haulers both haul things. They also both move them. But to Sam's mind the distinction was crystal: Things that people want or care about are moved. Things that people don't want or care about are hauled.

In some towns the Two Men And A Truck company is a franchise, the kind of place that hires buff frat boys and deducts FICA. This Two Men And A Truck was just that, two men and a pickup, just like Sam and Jeremy, the F-150, and Brotherman's Hauling. Sam and Jeremy might even have welcomed their expansion, a little competition, had those fuckers not tacked their flyers up directly over the Brotherman's flyers.

Sam took one of the tear-off phone numbers from the Two Men flyer. He then called with a fake hauling job. "It's a little drive out of town," he said. "But the payoff is worth it."

"We have a few moving gigs scheduled," one of the Two Men said. "If it's that big we can cancel them."

Sam described the job to him. The job he pitched was a point-by-point description of the first hauling job Brotherman's had ever done, transporting 500 80-gallon drums, the kind bums make fires in, to the barrel refurbishing plant. The plant's drivers had gone on a strike. It had required precision stacking, four-inch truck cargo straps, and multiple trips to haul it all in the F-150. But it had paid extremely well. That one job funded the whole business. It bought Brotherman's computer and the mobile. Sam described the job to the one man, who sounded very eager. Sam gave him a fake address of a drum processing facility on the Old Highway. He gave him a fake phone number too.

So when the mobile buzzed later that evening he didn't think anything much of it. Sam's plans have simple flaws. It was actually the two men of Two Men on at the same time.

"You cost us a day, pussboy," said one of them, Sam thought the same one he talked to earlier.

"A day," said the other one.

"That's Brotherman to you," Sam said. "You have conference call or something? How do you get that?"

"Yeah, we got conference call," said the first one. "And you got a genuine problem."

"What are they saying?" Jeremy said.

"They say we've got a problem," Sam said.

"Talking to your pussy, dick?" one of the two men said. Sam couldn't tell them apart anymore.

"They ask if I'm talking to my pussy," Sam said.

"Tell them your pussy takes umbrage at their comment," Jeremy said.

"Takes what?" Sam said.

"You guys need to watch your backs. This ain't cool. We let you run your little show around here long enough. Now there may be some action."

"An equal and opposite reaction?" Sam said in the voice of a black man imitating a white man.

"*Um-bridge*," Jeremy said.

"Payback action," the two men said.

"My pussy takes umbrage at your comment," Sam said.

"Umbrage *to* your comment," one of them said, and they hung up.

Sam regretted making the phony call.

"Well?" Jeremy said.

"They corrected you."

"Corrected what?"

"They said it's umbrage *to* your comment."

"Bullshit," Jeremy said. "Bullfuckingshit."

Sam is hyperaware of his shit as it moves through him. He searches the bowl. He probes with a wire coat hanger, but there's no penny. He feels it still, somewhere within him, a point of pressure there above his stomach, a little insignificant weight.

He removes two bowls of hot sauce from the fridge and soaks his fingers for ten minutes like he's seen women in manicure shops soaking their fingers. When time is up, he drip-dries over the bowls. The tips turn a crusty orange. They sting and tighten.

Today the hot sauce serves a double preventative purpose. Because the floors in Sam's apartment are paper-thin, the Red-haired Girl downstairs can hear him masturbating at his computer. Yesterday, the Red-haired Girl had a little talk with him during which he pretty much got the picture. She knocked on his door while he had the news on. She told him the news was too loud.

"It's the news," he said. "How can the news be loud?"

"I can hear everything that goes on up here," she said. "*Everything.*" This being her subtle hint that he might want to check the volume at which he engages Internet porn. He understood that she issued her complaint intentionally during an innocent moderate-volume news moment so as to get her point across when he was not in the middle of the activity she really wanted to put a stop to. She was smart, he figured. Of course he knew how troubling it was to be able to hear something like that. He could hear the guy above him jerking off to Internet porn too.

Some queerbaits might find the guy above you jerking off at the same time as you exciting. It really bugs Sam though. And because he can never hear the Red-haired Girl downstairs doing anything, he knows the guy upstairs can not hear him. Sound moves downward, he thinks.

So when he breaks for attempting to expel the penny again, he hears the guy upstairs watching *The Price Is Right* at a normal volume—normal in this building means, in the quiet of his apartment one floor removed, he hears the sound of Bob Barker's voice over his own bathroom fan.

Sam goes upstairs and knocks on the door. He keeps

his hands in his pockets.

"Hey neighbor," the guy says. "Why the eye patch?" They have never spoken before.

"Work injury," Sam says.

"Workman's comp. That's my secret." He grabs his thigh and says, "Oh my leg!" He hops around in his foyer. "If you know what I mean."

Sam delivers the exact same lines the Red-haired Girl used on him, and the guy upstairs responds at first pretty much as he had.

"Loudness is a subjective thing," the guy says.

"I can hear everything that goes on up here," Sam says. "*Everything.*" He tries to approximate the Red-haired Girl's expression. And he thinks the guy upstairs gets it, just as he had gotten it. Unlike Sam though, he pushes.

"Give me an example?" the guy says.

"Oh, I can, you know, just about everything. You walking around. Opening the refrigerator, listening to music, the boob tube."

"Like what? What was I watching at two a.m. this morning?"

"I don't actually log," Sam says.

"Sure you're not just an asshole?" the guy asks, sincerely Sam thinks.

"No, look, it's just that these apartments suck. I can hear everything all right."

"To travel, sound requires a medium of transmission. For instance, solid, liquid, or air. I suppose I could convert my apartment into a vacuum of space. There is no sound in a vacuum of space," the guy says.

Sam goes back downstairs. In a little while, just as Sam

is thinking about quietly jerking off, the guy upstairs starts in. He clearly isn't trying to hold it down any. Sam can hear him talking to the monitor. Sam blushes, picturing the Red-haired Girl hearing him saying very similar things.

Instead Sam sends out emails to old clients, offering them Proven Customer Discounts. *You Know Who to Call, When You Need a Haul: Brotherman's*, he writes at the end of each. Most of them come back asking to please have their addresses purged from this list. Many simply write, *remove*. The guy upstairs orgasms. He goes off like a bear. There is brief silence, then Bob Barker's muffled voice fills the room.

Sam eats a Pepcid and goes outside to walk around the apartment complex with his hands behind his head to try and get rid of the cramp coming on in his gut. The bad thing about the Red-haired Girl is that she has a dog, an ugly little English bulldog named Lusya. She walks it constantly with all the other women in the complex who have dogs. She's told them about Sam. He imagines her telling them about him going at it up there, three to four solid hours. Every woman with a dog in the complex avoids him. When he walks past them in the halls they look at the floor and allow their menacing dogs to the farthest reaches of their leashes, close enough to feel their hot breath on his marinated fingers.

The Red-haired Girl, however, being complicated, does talk to him. She has this nice thing. She wanted to let him know that she could hear what he was doing by telling him she could hear him doing something else, in order to get him to stop doing what he was doing so loudly, but in a way so he thought she really didn't hear what he was doing, because that kind of embarrassed her. And when she sees him with the patch over his eye, she feigns concern. He doesn't know her name and she doesn't know his.

He keeps his hands in his pockets—women notice hands—and tells her that he scratched the cornea at work. It's funny, he thinks, the loss of an eye doesn't really even bother him; the addition of a penny does. When they talk, while it is obvious she is trying to be nice, she maintains a nervous glance in her eye. Sam wonders if she has this with everyone. Lusya donates a half-hearted jump at his leg. Even her dog pretends to like him.

Evolutionarily speaking Sam considers himself a fluke. He is short, not tall. Like his fingernails, his toenails are bad, though he has never bitten them. He is not particularly smart; is weird looking; and no good at sports or fighting. He compulsively has bad idea after bad idea, such as starting this hauling company now dying a brisk death. There's not much propulsion behind his orgasm.

"You were right you know," he says. "These apartments really do suck. I mean. I don't know if I should tell you this. But the guy upstairs from me..." Sam leans toward her. "I don't know if I should tell you this."

"Yeah," she says, and steps backward.

"He masturbates all day," Sam says. He takes his hands out of his pockets but resists the urge to use the universal hand signal for jerking off. "For hours and hours. It's so loud."

"Are you kidding me?" she says.

"No. It's terrible, like he's in the same room with me, which you have to admit if you've ever seen him, it's a scary thought. But I don't want to go up there and tell him I can hear that, you know."

"Yeah, it's awkward, or something."

"You're telling me. I wouldn't be a bit surprised if you

could hear him straight through to your apartment."

"Hours and hours and hours?" she says.

"At least. And talking to the screen. *Oh baby, oh yeah baby.* It's enough to, I tell you. Freaking pathetic. I've heard him—and you know he's the only one up there—going *Rock with me. Rock with me. Suckle, suckle...*"

"I have in fact. Well, talk about embarrassing. I thought that was you." Her skin turns the exact shade of her hair and freckles, causing her freckles to temporarily disappear.

"Oh, no. No! You should—you can come up some time and listen. I mean just to prove it."

She immediately gets all apologetic. Her skin color deepens and deepens until it begins to brown. The shade of her skin overtakes the freckles and they resurface. She checks him out, seems to see him in a new light. She leans in, as if they're chuckling a secret. The dog rubs its butt against his boot.

"Do you smell hot sauce?" she asks.

There is an immediate, marked transformation in the way women with dogs around the complex relate to Sam. When he leaves that afternoon to pick up Jeremy, a blonde with a Newfoundland the size of a Yugo, a dog which she'd just yesterday allowed to plant both its front paws on his chest as he backed into a corner, waves hello at him, and when the Yugo goes for his hands, she jerks it back. "He's nothing," she says, "an absolute vagina monologue."

So Sam is as upbeat as a guy with a foreign body in him can be until they cruise around town checking their flyers. They discover all of them—at the gas stations, the COTA stops, the dump, the post office, fish camp, the industrial parks, in the Port-O-Lets at construction sites,

Skyline Chili, Payless Shoes, the comic book store—covered up with Two Men And A Truck flyers. They append their flyers with super sticky double-sided tape, which ruins the Brotherman's flyers underneath.

"The miracle is we still have enough pennies to Xerox our own flyers," Jeremy says when they check the Community Bulletin Board at the PriceChopper, "with you going around eating them all." Jeremy scribbles on the Two Men flyers. On one he draws a little caricature of two stick-figure men buttfucking in parentheses. On others he writes: *I take umbrage AT your two frigging faces. I take umbrage AT your hauling. I take umbrage TO the Two Fags And A Buckity-Buck.*

"You're not getting what I'm saying," Sam says. "It worked. I should have blown that breath reader off the charts. All the tequila I put back. It could have been fifty percent I'm telling you."

"With your drunk driving ability then, it had to have been the signs. Just take off the signs." Jeremy knows what a terrible drunk driver Sam is, but, knowing what pride Sam takes in his supposed prowess, he keeps it quiet and never goes out for the serious drinking with him after work. The truth is Jeremy has been talking to some guys at the dump who haul things around the landfill about bringing him on. There is no shortage of things people don't want at the dump like there seems to be in the rest of the world.

"I'm not talking about why I got pulled over. That seems pretty obvious. I'm saying the penny fucked up the test."

Jeremy staples the new Brotherman's flyers over the defaced Two Men flyers.

"I don't know anything about a breathalyzer, brotherman. Or for that matter what a penny will do about it. What I know is if you'd blown one one-thousandth more, there'd be no business right about now. Then what would we do?" Jeremy would step up the pressure on the guys at the dump is what. Jeremy can't drive, but can the bitch haul. The guy is built like a small forklift. When not carrying anything he moves about as if he's falling backwards. He slants at forty-five degrees from knees to waist. He's five foot four with arms that bear hug a Barcalounger. When he picks something up he sinks into himself; it's the only time his feet and head are in line. Sam interprets these qualities to mean that Jeremy can fight.

Jeremy can haul. Jeremy likely intimidates. Jeremy cannot fight.

"If one single person on one single night sees these signs, and we get a job out of it, that's one job more we'd have than now. I'm not taking off the signs. I'd just like to pass this penny."

"It will pass," Jeremy says. "Have faith in that much."

Sam doesn't know.

Once they replace their fliers they do what they usually do: They buy a six-pack of Hollandia tall boys and go drink them at the park with their feet propped on the rear-view mirrors. The end of Brotherman's may be near anyway. Jeremy hands Sam his hot sauce from the glove compartment, and he upturns it into his beer. He drinks the beer in hopes it will make him feel normal.

They wait for the mobile to ring. Jeremy searches phrase books and novels and newspapers from the library for passages quoting *umbrage at* something. Periodically he steps out and does pull-ups on the jungle gym. Sam worries about the penny and tries not to chew his nails. He rubs under his rib cage to see if he can feel anything and stains his T-shirt orange.

"You're worth more now," Jeremy says. "Think of it like that. Sam plus one cent." Then Jeremy says, "Tomorrow, let's go in early and ambush the Two Men at PriceChopper." Sam understands this to mean they will be kicking some Two Men ass in retribution for having one of their cop buddies pull him over, but Jeremy intends only to clarify a grammatical point.

"What time?" Sam says.

"Early, make sure we don't miss them," he says.

"Sixish then?"

"Sixish."

Sam purchases sample packs of Metamucil and Ex-Lax and a single packet of apple and cinnamon oatmeal from the Dollar Store on the way home. That night he panics the panic of a man who may have something seriously wrong with him medically but does not have insurance. His jowls quiver. He's sweaty and pale in the bathroom mirror, white as the gauze eye patch. He washes his hands and he wants to bite them so bad they tremble. He rushes into the kitchen and soaks them again in the two bowls of hot sauce, beating his head on the table to the *Jeopardy* tune. He mixes fiber, oatmeal, and laxative in a bowl of boiling water. He breathes the steam, and when it's cool enough he eats.

Afterward he powers on the computer and finds a yellow plastic glove for dishwashing under the sink. He coats it in Vaseline, goes to one of the free movie sites and cranks up. He talks to the screen, imitating the voice of the guy upstairs, and when it's over he collapses into the lawn chair he uses as an office chair, then spends an hour on the toilet pushing, concentrating, pushing, before admitting failure, swallowing half a Xanax and falling deeply to sleep.

The Red-haired Girl hears Sam as she prepares for bed and watches the Weather Channel, slightly concerned by the

TV's constant beeping because of severe incoming weather. She believes that it is the guy two floors up jerking off while talking to the screen, even though the sound seems to be coming from directly over her head. The walls and ceilings are thin enough, she believes, which is why the severe incoming weather concerns her.

Sam wakes to weather sirens and the taste of vinegary fingers. In his sleep, the fingers of his left hand—his favorite to chew for reasons having to do with angle and bent—have migrated to his mouth. Outside it sounds like a bombing raid. He opens his window and the wind and rain whip through the room. Sirens are interspersed with a garbled message. He sticks his head out into the dark to hear better. Weather-warning megaphone speakers in the distance blare something that sounds like: *Lorena Bobbitt in area. Seek lover.*

He can barely hear knocking at the door. It's the Red-haired Girl, standing there holding a vanilla-scented candle.

"This is your wake-up call," she says. "The severe incoming weather is income. The whole building's in the basement."

Sam disappears to find his shoes. He slips his bare feet into his work boots. When he comes back she is standing in his living room. In the lightning flashes, he sees the hot sauce bowls on the kitchen table, the open tub of Vaseline and the glove on the computer desk.

"We have the exact same space," she says. "And there is where the magic happens." She points to the ceiling.

He makes to get her out of the room fast, taking her by the waist. She interprets this as a forward move. She likes forward. They take the steps carefully in the dark, stopping only to let the guy upstairs brush by with a flashlight, his feet smacking the stairs like soft tomatoes.

The Red-haired Girl enters the basement first. Her

candle illuminates their neighbors and a goldmine of junk. Sam simply marvels for a moment. The remnants of who knows how many years of tenants' leftovers, rotten and mildewed from the moisture, well beyond any desirable condition. The mess is arranged in aisles. Their neighbors are situated among the aisles in little cliques. The women with dogs smile nervously and wave. Every person secretly chastises himself for saving the however-much per month to live in the flimsy-walled apartment building they all live in. An AM radio reports multiple tornadoes spotted in the area.

Sam takes the candle and the lead now. He wanders through lanes of wooden crates, old doors, paintings, battered suitcases, porch swings, mattresses, and box springs. There's ancient dressers and stacks of mismatched drawers, a foreign-looking shrunk, and couch beds—big, heavy, steel couch beds.

The Red-haired Girl takes Sam's arm. Her nails dig into his bicep. He registers their crispy quality. He looks down and is excited to find that he can see them reflecting the candle, finely shaped, perfectly manicured, the kind with a whitewall across the top and a lavender body. The Xanax emphasizes everything.

The Red-haired Girl stops him in front of a basement window. She points to a blanket underneath two sawhorses, where her bulldog Lusya is sitting. "Kind of a cool spot right?" she says.

"A room with a view," Sam says. Through the window they see the little shrubs lining the apartment building sideways in the wind.

The siren and the unintelligible announcement broken-records.

"What the hell are they trying to tell us?" Sam asks.

"The sky is plummeting," she says.

"I don't know your name," Sam says.

"You see me all the time," she says.

"I call you the Red-haired Girl," Sam says.

"You're the Creepy Cute Guy!" she says. "Let's just stick with those." Then she says, "Look." The little sideways shrubs are gone.

When he wakes up, he is horrified to discover his hand clawing up the Red-haired Girl's stockinged leg, catching and running as it goes. A purple light seeps in through the window, and the basement is quiet.

She interprets his gesture in a particular way and pulls herself out of the shredded stockings.

"Touch me," she says. Sam retracts his hands out of habit.

"I don't do touch," Sam says. She interprets this in a particular way also. Sam is really shy and awkward about these things. She interprets him as forceful and direct.

She says something else then, which Sam cannot decipher: "Moose me," maybe.

Sam does what he believes is expected of him. He is intrigued to discover she tastes like lemon. Leaned against the foreign shrunk in the back corner the guy upstairs begins masturbating, for the first time in his life, quietly, without even a whisper as he watches them through the sawhorses.

Soon Sam desires different textures. He bites, which seems to be the thing. Her body flops around. He keeps on biting, all the way down her leg, her ankle for a while, back up, knee, hip bone, nipple one, nipple two, lip, ear, lymph node, neck fold. She goes for it. When he moves down her arm—shoulder, elbow, wrist—something tells him just to get what it is he's after. He starts small, the hard, tender nail on the end of her pinky. He nips that off in two clean bites, no tearing, practiced. Then goes the thumb. He decimates her lovely nails, during which she orgasms thrice.

The Red-haired Girl, while genuinely liking this, does not however expect that it will constitute the main activity of a sexual relationship with Sam. The guy upstairs finishes all over himself, without making a sound.

Sam would say that he notices the penny less today. But no one is asking. Jeremy is writing on a piece of paper as Sam maneuvers the F-150 through the twilight, around fallen power lines and trees, to the PriceChopper. He parks at the other end of the parking lot, away from the automatic doors, where they have a clear view of the Community Bulletin Board.

Six-thirty rolls around and then seven. Sam calls the landlord on the mobile. He explains to him that he just happened to seek shelter in the basement last night and couldn't help noticing all the junk. He also just happens to run a hauling company if he's interested in getting rid of it. The landlord seems receptive, asks for the name of his business. There is a negotiating period. Sam wants two months' rent. The landlord says he'll meet him there to discuss it further this week, but right now, he could actually use Brotherman's to haul away the detritus tornados dropped onto a number of his properties. Sam says he thinks they could find time in their schedules to do that today.

"We got work," he says, turning to Jeremy. Jeremy is too nervous to answer.

A truck parks in the fire lane.

Sam and Jeremy look at each other. They get out. The Two Men—caught taping over their flyers—notice them from across the parking lot. They recognize the duo from having themselves once staked out the competition for the same purpose they are now being staked out. When they'd seen Jeremy, they'd called that plan off. Now they come toward them, full stride.

And this is when Jeremy stops. Sam stops too, figuring that Jeremy is bearing the brunt of this thing.

Jeremy holds up the piece of paper he's been working on and clears his throat. The Two Men eye them from across the parking lot like in an old Western. Jeremy begins to read:

"Mr. Jack Maldon shook hands with me; but not very warmly, I believed; and with an air of languid patronage, at which I secretly took great umbrage…A wife…who properly conducted her economy, should take no umbrage at such little fancies of her husband, but be always certain that he would return…"

Sam ignores what he thinks he mistakenly perceives as a tremble in Jeremy's voice. He is not mistaken.

"How fathers should not draw too ready rein/Nor sons take umbrage in a trice/At father's counsels…"

Sam recognizes fully the miscalculation made here when the Two Men recommence their approach and the sound of footsteps in hasty retreat appears first from beside him, where Jeremy was just a moment ago standing, reciting his speech, then from further and further behind him. On his stocky legs, Jeremy trucks through the parking lot. He moves well through the morning. Sam wonders where exactly he plans to go. Jeremy figures he was on his way out anyhow.

The Two Men stand in front of Sam.

"There's so many things you can do with a truck," he offers.

Just one of the Two Men, the one who *looks* like he used to be a cop, takes his shot, which Sam manages to block, but then the other hand of the one Two Men comes out of nowhere because the eye patch makes for this huge blind spot. Sam stays where he falls on the wet asphalt. His teeth feel pushed. His mouth, drowned in blood, tastes of penny.

The Two Men look down on him as the grocery store cop waltzes over.

"This poor guy's keeling here," says one of the Two Men.

"Must of just fell," one of them said.

"Must of," says the other.

They both high-five the cop.

He dreams about the Red-haired Girl's fingernails. In the dream he vividly experiences the crack as they snap between his teeth...to gauge he puts his own thumb in his mouth and pushes around on his teeth. They are all there, but the front ones give, roughly as much play as the steering wheel on the F-150...the cop returns with a fat man dressed in grocery store manager clothes. They look down at him. "Might be he's a vagrant," the cop says. "Hey," the manager says. "You speak English? No loitering."

For a little while Sam has all at the same time a scratched cornea, a penny impacted in his esophagus, and a mild concussion. Not to mention loose teeth. A nurse has coated his fingernails in iodine interpreting them as injuries based on their assumption that he's homeless. He tells him about the penny. Then he's in the radiology suite and the doctor is cramming a balloon down his throat (fluoroscopic balloon catheter extraction), then inflating the balloon (which is like taking a deep breath without taking the breath), and pushing the penny into his stomach.

They put him in a bed next to a kid who has swallowed a small light bulb. They apparently group like injuries together in emergency rooms. They want to keep him there for a couple hours, and since no one has brought up the whole insurance thing yet he doesn't talk too much. If they figure he's a charity case let them figure he's a charity case. The kid keeps hogging the bathroom in their area to vomit. And after one trip he emerges smiling and holding a little unbroken bulb between his thumb and index finger.

When Sam takes his turn, he has what you would consider to be your standard, normal bowel movement. There is no plink, nor any feeling like you might expect with a penny coming out of your ass. He does not even think he's expelled it, but he checks anyway, and there it is submerged in the bottom of the pot. It seems larger and shinier than he'd expected. Sam has never seen a penny so bright and shiny.

He uses the back end of the toilet scrubber to slide it up the porcelain. Once he gets it near the rim he reaches in and peels it off. He washes the penny and his hands under the cool water from the hospital sink. He dries off with the thick paper towels and holds the penny up to the fluorescent light.

In that light Sam catches sight of his fingernails. Underneath the hot sauce and iodine they are beginning to grow over, maybe for the first time, with small but definite frosty white tips, still jagged but smoothing. The trajectory is clear. They will grow up and through the inflamed pink cuticle. They will have to. There is nowhere else to go. This will be painful, but the final result is something that Sam wants to admire. He wants to see that. For the time being at least, he thinks, I am holding in my hands eleven accomplishments.

An Evening of Jenga®

" FOUNDATION," VADIM SAID. "BASE," HE SAID.

"When it gets right down to it," I said, "if you're taking middles, you're encumbering a piece is what you're doing."

"Okay," he said, "I'm glad you're not an architect."

"Vadim, allow me to enlighten your Russian ass: Skyscrapers sway. Did you know that skyscrapers sway, Vadim? Why is it do you think that skyscrapers sway? They sway because they are flexible, and flexible structures are *less* likely to fall."

"Bad analogy. Jenga isn't a building. It's a game in which one must, on occasion, take middles."

"That wasn't an analogy," Inna said. "That was a statement."

"I thought we were going somewhere for dessert, babe," Liza said.

"Bad statement," Vadim said.

"Let's just play one more game, the four of us. Come on. It'll be fun."

"Hand me that level," Vadim said. He put it on the table beside the tower. "Satisfied?"

"Bring this side up another tick," I said.

Vadim tapped a wood chip under the table leg with a riveting hammer, and I said, "Stop. Perfecto."

"Cheesecake," Liza said, "is fun."

Vadim's retarded brother Bipkus pounded on the wall, which is how he asks for more pizza. They keep Bipkus locked in his room whenever we're over so he doesn't creep everybody out.

"His Lowness calls," Inna said but didn't move. Then someone knocked on the front door and she scurried across the hardwood floor.

"Mehmet," she said. "You came."

"I forgot to tell you about this guy," Vadim said.

Mehmet came in. He's scrawny but with a hard face, the skin on his nose and cheeks the texture of bricks. Inna told him to grab some pizza. She dabbed grease off a piece then delivered it into Bipkus's room. "Want your tip, lady?" Bipkus said to her. "Don't eat yellow snow."

"You're welcome," Inna said, "you turbid shit."

Vadim's ears turned red and he said to Mehmet, "Hey, neighbor, come and get your Jenga on."

"Where are you from?" Liza asked Mehmet.

"Turkey," he said.

"Mehmet moved here after his family died," Inna said.

"Maybe you heard about this," he said, "big earthquake."

"An earthquake," I said.

"Yes," he said. "How do you play?"

"We're trying to build this tower as high as we can," I said. "The person who knocks it down loses."

"The best one to start with," Vadim said, "is this one right here." He poked out the bottom middle. It skidded across the table and landed on the soft white carpet. I shook my head.

"When was the earthquake?" Inna asked.

"We thought the whole world was crackling to pieces," Mehmet said. "I was under a hot tub—I worked in a hot tub store. It was the only thing that saved me."

"A hot tub," I said.

Liza took a middle and smiled at me. Bipkus sang Kid Rock into his karaoke machine behind his closed bedroom door.

Inna said, "Vadim."

"Sorry guys," Vadim said. "He's bored."

"Tell him to come out," Liza said. She looked at Inna.

"I'm so happy to have my own bathroom. It's like I have my own life again," Inna said. She bobbed a grape from the glass of sangria.

"Hey buddy," Vadim shouted. "Can you cut that shit out?"

Bipkus screamed, "Bah wit da wah." He turned up the volume on the karaoke machine.

"Isn't it Bah wit da *bah*?" I said.

"I don't understand this song," Vadim said.

Mehmet reached for the tower. From the bottom row, which was already missing its middle, he pulled a side. It capsized. A block bounced into Liza's sangria glass and it spilled onto the white carpet. Mehmet held the block stupidly where the tower just was.

"Let me clean it with something," said Mehmet. He carefully placed the block on the table.

Liza told him no, she'd get it, but Inna told her to sit down. Inna got up, came back with the pitcher of sangria, and refilled Liza's glass.

"We're not even going to bother cleaning," Inna said. She sat back down and started rebuilding the tower. "Living here with"—she pointed at Bipkus's room. "Living here with this person is living with stain. One more won't kill us."

"That's not fair, hon," Vadim said. "You know, he's my brother."

Inna pressed her finger into the middle of the red blotch then looked at her finger, licked it.

"I'm sorry," Mehmet said. "It's a hard game."

"Didn't take much physics did you?" I say. "I'm just kidding. Listen. That was an impossible move. If there's three blocks making up the row, and the middle one's gone. You can't take either side. That row's done. Similarly, if one or both side is gone, you can't take a middle. See what I'm saying?"

"It's the nature of a disagreement between us," Vadim said. "The object of the game is to build the tower as high as possible without knocking it down. So there's this constant negotiation between sturdiness and potential height. My friend thinks that you should never take a middle, but, see, that makes for a teetering tower. Every five or so levels, you need a stable one, and you get a stable one by taking a middle."

"Look, Mehmet, speaking of obvious, if you're going for height, you don't take middles. Unfortunately some people don't subscribe to the Theory of the Obvious."

"Thank you, Herb, for The American Perspective," Vadim said. He poured glasses of vodka for the three men.

"It is just a game, boys," Liza said.

"I think that I am now getting this," Mehmet said.

"Can we go get dessert now?"

Inna finished stacking but the walls were uneven. Vadim trued it with the straightedge. I went first, taking a bottom side.

"Liza, you're a sweet girl," Vadim said. "If it was Liza, I know Liza would accept your brother in her home. If you had a brother like Bipkus, Herb, she would take him in and things, like little things, he did that were kind of weird she would just accept because he's your brother. I swear, you know, I love Inna." He reached under the glass table and touched her foot. "But if I didn't have Inna, and you weren't with Herb, I would fall in love with you, Liza. I'm just saying.

"Seriously, you guys are our best friends," Vadim said. "I wanted to tell you that. Even you, Mehmet. Collectively you make up one unit of best friendedship. You plural are our best friend. We mean that. Let's drink a toast."

We clinked glasses. Vadim poured more vodka, and Liza took an easy middle from right in the center of the tower.

Mehmet stared at the tower for a long time. We drank vodka and sangria while we waited. Vadim tried to show him which ones were easy.

"See," Vadim said, "like these." He illustrated. He poked casually at middles up and down the tower. Then he poked them all back in. I didn't say anything about the middles even though there were sides that would come out just as smooth.

Mehmet nodded.

"And it's just a game," Liza said. "Don't worry so much."

Mehmet hovered his finger near the center of the tower. He moved his head around like a praying mantis.

"What do you mean by that, *it's just a game?*" I asked Liza. "I don't really understand what you're trying to get at by saying that all the time."

"I mean we're playing something. There's no deep meaning behind it."

"If it's just a game, then why do you always take middles?"

"I take middles, Herb, because they're the easiest ones to take."

"It's funny," I said. "If you really thought it was just a game, wouldn't it be rather coincidental that you always take the pieces that I believe shouldn't be taken? Wouldn't you just once take a side, for variety?"

"Middles are easier. I like easy. But if I really thought, I would think that I want some dessert."

"It is a game and it isn't," Inna said.

Mehmet dropped his hand to the bottom row, poking out the load-bearing middle, and the tower crashed to the table.

"I am sorry," he said, blushing. "It is difficult one." He went to the bathroom.

My normal mode: Take world as literally as possible, observe each action, hear words, respond when response is necessary. Resist ponder. Repeat.

After the second time Mehmet knocked down the tower, I began to do something I don't normally do until more vodka: I thought. I thought, *What the fuck? Here I am,* I thought, *in a room full of foreigners, including my wife. And this guy is trying to fuck with me and my country with this game.*

"Who the hell is this guy?" I said.

"He smokes by the dumpster," Inna said.

"Do tits fly in Turkey?" I said. "Does gravity operate? Did you move to the all-immigrant complex?"

"Don't be rude," Liza said. "It's almost eleven."

"No, I heard about this," Vadim said. "There was like this coal mine in one of these southern places or Africa, and they wanted the native workers or whatever to pick up the coal when it fell out of the carts. They didn't speak the language though and they didn't have people who spoke the language. Don't ask me how they got them to work. Don't ask me how. They made this little comic, like a poster but with comic frames, and it showed a guy reaching down and picking up a piece of coal and putting it in the cart. Of course...we read left to right. These people read right to left. So they started taking the coal out of the carts and dropping it on the ground. Cultural relativism. I shit you not."

Bipkus emerged and kicked at the bathroom door. We heard Mehmet saying something but none of us could tell if he was saying, "Mehmet, Mehmet" or "minute, minute."

"Hey buddy," Vadim said. "It's our across-the-hall neighbor in there."

Inna put her face in her hands.

"Ba wit da wah," Bipkus said. He drooled. He needed not drool, but he turns the retarded on when there's company.

"Just give him a minute. He'll be done in a minute. Have some more pizza. Help yourself."

Bipkus looked around the corner at us. "Oh, hey, Herb, Liza." He disappeared and the door to his room slammed shut.

Inna scraped the backs of her fingernails underneath her chin.

"Inna," Vadim said, "when we decided to bring Bipkus

over we knew—"

"*We* decided to bring Bipkus over?"

"Inna," Vadim said, "we've discussed it. He's my brother."

She laughed and sipped the sangria. "Teasing. I love cleaning piss out of the bathroom sink."

"You want to do this in front of our friends?" Vadim said. "Inna is still adjusting to living with Bipkus," he said to us. "This space is helping."

Mehmet came out of the bathroom and looked strangely at us.

"Sorry, neighbor. My brother. He's demanding about his bathroom."

Bipkus threw open the door and blew by Mehmet into his bathroom.

"It's I should be sorry," Mehmet said. He's smirking, I thought.

"No way," Vadim said. "One more game. We're getting this thing right."

I built the tower up that time. I described in plain language the spaces that open up in the crevices between the blocks. "The weight shifts," I said to Mehmet, "and certain ones come out at certain times and certain other ones at certain other times."

"You actually look more retarded than your retarded brother," Inna said to Vadim. This is something that Inna had said before about her husband to me when she was drunk.

"Inna," Liza said.

I guided Mehmet's hand—the skin was brown and smooth and hotter than I'd expected—and slid out a side. Mehmet stationed it at the top of the tower. Liza and I erupted in applause.

"If we stood you next to Bipkus in a line-up for retards, you'd get picked over him hands down," Inna said. "Your face is oblong. One side of your head is like an old balloon."

Vadim took a middle in silence. Bipkus pounded on the wall.

Mehmet's hand flashed toward the remaining bottom block, but my hand was faster. I snagged his wrist.

"Don't do it, motherfucker. There are no hot tubs here to protect you from the Earthquake of Herb."

"What are you doing?" Liza said. "How much did he drink?"

"Herb, let him go," Vadim said.

"I'm not letting him go, Vadim." I tightened my grip. "Correction, you want me to let him go, you ask him this question for me. Go ahead and ask him. Ask him if he's knocking this tower down on purpose. Ask him if he's trying to say something. Ask him."

"Say what, Herb, what is everyone trying to say?" Liza said.

"I have a pretty good idea," I said.

"Sir, please, release my arm," Mehmet said.

"You're being too touchy, Herb," Vadim said. "It's an interpretation."

"It's a little—it's not so fun for me," I said.

"Come on, Herb, he's just playing around," Liza said.

"Liza, if you tell me that we're just playing or that this is just a game one more time or just this or just that, I'm going to leave you here. I'm going to leave and just leave you here."

"I am sorry, Herbs, I am only not good at games," Mehmet said.

Mehmet stood and I stood too, not letting him go, our arms locked over the tower in what surely seemed to Bipkus, as he emerged, an awkward handshake.

"Your politics lack a certain subtlety," I said.

Bipkus approached and covered our hands with his huge palm. "Go teams," he said, bopping our hands hard enough to bust them apart then raising his in the air for high-fives. He does look normal, I thought. Mehmet and I high-fived him. He carried a box of pizza into his room and slammed the door shut again.

We sat down on the floor cushions.

I turned to Vadim. "It's not just meanness," I said. "She believes what she's said." We looked at Inna who had her finger in the sangria blotch again.

"Dessert," Liza said. "Dessert is requisite before the end of the night."

"I know," Vadim said. "That's what kills."

The Boy and the Colgante

FOR AN EXTERNAL OUTDOOR FLAGPOLE, ONE NEED not necessarily go with the Illuminator Hurricane Series, to wit a flagged wind speed of 220 miles per hour-plus, if one is not in, say, Florida. And I am nowhere near Florida. I am in what Floridians think of as the anti-Florida if they think of a place like this, if they even know about what might exist not a few hours north of the Vermont border of the United States of America. I *wish* for Florida.

I am in Roberval, Quebec, Canada, the long-distance swimming capital of the world, a place to wit there are creatures heretofore unbeknown to me which is called a French Redneck. The French Redneck is very much like the American Redneck we know and love but for the obvious fact it speaks French. I will not even tell you how I landed here other than to inuit (which is a kind of indian here) to the fact that it is on account of the boy, that lacking-in-character son

of mine, who loves America not even enough to put his butt
on the line for it, who because I love him enough to put my
butt on the line for him have put it so. I am now here and am
technically considered an accomplice by the laws of the good
country which I love should I ever return which I can't see
because how would it look to the people who share my views
and whose sons are not lacking in character? To wit there are
days I have no idea what I am doing here. It is an uninteresting
and unfortunate little tale. I'll spare you.

One does not necessarily need go with the Illuminator
Hurricane Series, flagged wind speed of 220 miles per hour-
plus, but I am going with it. I am installing a 50-foot exposed
height, 10-inch diameter butt, 4-inch diameter top, and while
this pole easily supports the 15 x 10 foot flag I am settling
for the 12 x 8 so as not to make the neighbors feel *too* bad,
which still will be tough because it's spun polyester, the most
durable flag material on the market, with sewn stripes and
embroidered stars. The beauty of the Illuminator, where
usually a regular flagpole top caps out, the Illuminator orbs a
fixture to wit powers a 120-volt halogen or 12-volt Zenon to
alight the whole shebang through the night, when it will flap
over this suburban Roberval neighborhood in a Zenon—I am
going with the Zenon—glow.

I am going with all this, because the flags
decorating—and that's just it, flags are symbols and idols
and not decoration—the French Redneck porches of every
house around us have begun to irritate me. They are of two
sorts, mostly the crimson zit of a maple leaf, *printed* mind
you on a nylon scrap, popping in the wind. The Quebec
flag I can stomach, four little reproductions of that thing,
reminds me of a Webelos badge, and at minimum cloth with

stitching. Got some symmetry. With that I can pert deal. I'm all right in general with Canada. Sure, the Maple Leafs. And then when they speak English it's all turned around. There's the *sawrys* and the way that the first *a* in two-*a* words gets backward. The *dra*ma of driving a *Maz*da. But I intend to make a statement this morning when the semi, an actual semi, comes down the street with the pole chained to the trailer and the flag folded down and boxed the size of a nice dining room table.

I have already dug and wired the hole and the boy is stirring six bags of Quickcrete in a wheelbarrel. Though he is not, as we say, altogether with the program, he understands that he owes me something here. The semi guys help us stand it in and run some support lines to the house and before long we are ceremoniously raising the flag of the US of A, flicking a switch and illuminating it just before dusk when the French Rednecks on all sides step off the porches, summoned like moths, except French-speaking and Canadian moths instead of the kind you would expect, so in about a round way they're like exactly what you would expect except different in some small and altogether disconcertive way.

After a few moments all of them are in my yard, standing next to me and the boy at the base of the Illuminator Hurricane, and they are all speaking in French. The boy talks to an Asian Redneck, who lives right next door. Imagine it, an Asian with maple leafs and Webelos all over his house, speaking perfect French. That is something.

"Ne *boo* play," I say. "What? What is it, boy?"

"They seem impressed," the boy says. "They say it's a fire hazard."

"That's Zenon," I say, "Less heat than Halogen. Emits."

The boy says something to them and the Asian French Redneck mouths the word "Zenon."

I mouth the words "Illuminator Hurricane, motherfucker."

The non-Asian French Redneck from the other side what knocks on my door at three am, saying something in frog.

"*Sawry*, eh?" I say. "*Sawry*."

He continues. The boy appears. Him and the non-Asian French Redneck talk. I can't tell you what they're saying, but I can say for fact that you can hear the country in the way a French Redneck talks. It's like yak butter or meat jelly. You don't know exactly what it is but you know it's there.

"He says the light from the flagpole is shining into his bedroom, Dad," the boy says.

I study the French Redneck. You can see in his eye the belief that everyone who ever did anything important in the world—invent electricity or the name for a dish of fries in gravy and cheese or the solid-body guitar or went to space, wiped out polio, sacrificed their line for braided-hair virgins—I imagine his belief that everyone who ever did any of those important things was French like him, just like blacks with blacks and Jews with Jews, Peruvians with Peruvians. The French Redneck looks like REO Speedwagon. He wears jeans that are too long on him and a Ducks Unlimited t-shirt. Has hairy toes. Drives a pickup.

He says another thing, and the boy doesn't translate.

"*Sawry*, eh," I say. I flick the porch switch, which the Illuminator is wired into.

The boy goes back to bed. I stand at the door until I hear the non-Asian French Redneck's front door close. Then I count off sixty seconds, just how long I reckon it takes him to get those jeans off and back cozy into bed. I flick the porch switch again and go to shower where we have this shower head that opens up to a monsoon and the water hits the tub with such force you can only barely make out the pounding on the door. But I have only my upper body soaped down when I notice something I can't believe I missed before. In the pocket corner of the showerhead we picked up from the dollar store just a few days un, there's a stamp in the metal: "Made in Tehran."

And suddenly I'm up in the sky, aught from space, seeing my own house with X-ray vision, the Illuminator casting a shadow of that gorgeous flapping flag down on my roof, and I see through all the Canadian-made shingles, to the bathroom where a turkey named me is standing in the shower, the water kept in by a curtain hung from a rod made in the place where my country is getting its war on next. I snatch it down and reach for my towel.

The boy and I are building a rock garden around the base of the Illuminator Hurricane the morning when the water meter reader comes down the drive. He speaks in French. The boy tries to step in, translate. I put my hand over his mouth.

"It's around back," I say. "But they just read the thing to wit a week ago."

"You don't speak French, sir?" he says.

"Dramamine," I say.

"Excuse me."

"I'm fluent beginner Canadia."

"I am here from city works. We received some complaints. And I'm sorry to say, but this, it's against see city code. It must come down." He looks up at the flag.

"That's the Illuminator Hurricane."

"Yes. I am afraid Robervale law is nothing in the residential region over eight meters."

"It's under eight."

"This is at least 15 meters, sir."

"You didn't measure it."

"I can measure it, if you like."

"I think you'll find it's under eight meters if you do."

The French city works guy stands there a moment before fishing a tape measure from his back pocket, stepping into my new rock garden and running it up the pole. I rake the red and brown and yellow maple leafs into a pile by the rock garden then sit on the rocks and one by one tear them along the veins, listening to the plinking of his metal tape measure on the Illuminator Hurricane.

"You see, sir, it is almost fifteen and a half."

"Oh, shit," I say. "I thought you meant feet. It said on the box it was under eight football fields, American football of course. I'm not Argonaut or Blue Bombering here. It's all confusing, but I don't think anyone minds."

"We are receiving many solicitations on this matter." A gust of wind whips the flag. "I am afraid it is the law and the rules. If you do not take it down, we will start to fine 150 dollars per day. It is an expensive rent for a flagpole."

"A hundred and fifty per? Let me think about that. Is that cash?"

I knew what this guy was thinking. But it wasn't that even. I'm just into the spectacular, and if anything in the world is not spectacular, it is a Canadian flag. Run one of them up this pole and it'll look all wrong flapping in the Zenon of the Illuminator. It just doesn't carry the weight. And that comes across I guess, which is why they're all after me about it.

"Let me ask you this: If I hang one of those maple leaf pus bubbles from this pole, can I keep it?"

"We are having laws here, sir. It is not a negotiable. But I may ask you, this is about genitalia? You have big American penis and this is how you show it to us all?" He smiles.

"I'm not going to accept that," I say. "I will take the Illuminator Hurricane down to avoid you fining me, but until my dick is 50 feet long with a queen-size flag draped off it, a Zenon bulb for a tip, you better take that back."

Me and the boy stand in the yard staring up at the Illuminator flagpole after the city guy leaves. The boy won't admit, but I can see that it stirs something in him too.

"Going down to a 25-footer isn't going to hurt us, Dad," the boy says.

"What is going to hurt us, boy?" I say. "Come on."

We drive to the dollar store.

To wit the boy makes a stupid point. You can't go down in size by half and expect it not to hurt you in dramatic effect. And I don't even know rightly if they make the Illuminator in 25-foot. And what then? Put floodlights on it from the roof overhang? Might as well cross the border and go to jail free. Maybe it's where we both belong.

I count the Canadian flags on porches and mailboxes and hanging off siding. They might be postage stamps as much as they're flags. Got zero meaning. A leaf is not a symbol. It's a picture, a drawing. At best you get nature off it. But you take an American flag and you know an American flag is in the room with you, or on the street with you, or in the neighborhood. You can *feel* an American flag, especially when presented all 50-foot Illuminator Hurricane and all.

At the dollar store, the boy wanders the aisles. I tell the woman straight off, "Ma'am, I am not speaking French with you. But I am returning this Iranian curtain rod on account of it's Iranian."

She seems puzzled, then twirls it behind the counter like a baton.

"No exchange."

"I don't want to exchange. I'm giving it back. Just take it. And accept my friendly customer-service suggestion to discontinue the stocking of this and all Tehran product."

"Made in Iran?" she says. Her co-worker comes over and they speak in French. Theirs is not redneck French. Something different. You can hear it in the expression.

The boy appears at my side. "What are you doing, Dad?"

"I'm returning this Iranian curtain rod."

"Why's it Iranian?"

"That's the most natural question you've asked in a time."

The woman points to the metal stamp on the rod and shows it to the boy.

"It says, 'Made in Taiwan,' Dad."

"What'd you say to me?" I have a look, hold it up to my face and pull it back. "Still don't want it." I drop it on the counter and walk out, wait for the boy in the car.

The boy drives. Little piles of snow form peaks on the sides of the road. He slips a CD out of his breast pocket. The CD has a metal ring through it, looped around a silver thread. The CD has an American flag print and the letters "USA." The bilingual packaging says "Hanging CD / CD Colgante."

"I got you something, Dad," he says. "It's not a 50-foot flagpole, I know."

"Some kind of decoration?" I say.

"It's only a decoration if you put it facing out. If it faces you, then it's just for you. All anyone else sees is the reflective back of a CD. Here."

He takes it out and hangs it over the mirror. We drive and it swings from the rear-view, slicing the air between us.

"What's *colgante* mean in frog?"

"It's Spanish. It means hanging, or pendant."

"Why's it Spanish."

"I don't know."

It was another stupid notion the boy had. It was clearly a decoration. But something about it endeared me to wit I respected its Spanish, the second language of the USA.

"Music on there?" I ask.

The boy shrugs. I pry the metal ring off the colgante with my side teeth. I feed it into the CD player and there's a long silence while the player tries to read it. The boy turns the volume knob all the way up and then it starts. The "Star Spangled Banner" played on little Mexican guitars, a maraca keeping the beat.

He turns it down, and I slap the back of his hand.

"Jam that colgante, boy!" I say.

We ride the streets like that, windows down so the cool air bites, the "Star Spangled Banner" playing on repeat. I picture myself busting up the cement base of the Illuminator Hurricane with the sledgehammer when we get home. I picture the boy, while I am busting, propping his feet on the sofa and eating what's called here a Wagon Wheel but is a Moon Pie. Though it seems to be my lot, bringing up things that in the end I will tear down, I start to feel a little good again, riding around like that, picturing only the immediate future, with the "Star Spangled Banner" cranking, with my boy and the colgante.

The Briefcase of the Pregnant Spylady

LET'S PLAY A GAME, HIS FATHER SAYS.

The game, Hryushka wants to say, a specific member of a group. But two things his father will never figure out: articles and customer service. So Hryushka says nothing. He goes and gets his scoop.

Six burlap sacks are prearranged in the old chest freezer they've converted into storage. The cooling fans no longer work, and Hryushka himself severed the power cord, which his father used to power a bucket that he turned into a leaf blower. Each sack contains a different granule: sugar, flour, salt, dog food, buckwheat, semolina. His father has sewn zippers into the sacks and locked them with little padlocks.

His father zips Hryushka along with his keychain flashlight and scoop into a seventh sack, then lifts him, with some difficulty, into the freezer and closes the lid. Hryushka's job, once zippered into the seventh sack and closed in the freezer, is to unzipper himself from the seventh sack, to jimmy the little padlock on the other sacks one-by-one, taking one scoop of granule from each, depositing it into a ziplock bag, rezipping and relocking each sack—if he breaks a little padlock while jimmying it he has to superglue it back together—then to rezipper himself, the keychain flashlight and scoop, and the six ziplocks of granule into the seventh sack.

He has done it so many times he no longer gets claustrophobic or breaks a sweat even when his father kicks the freezer, even when he tips it all the way over and then rights it. Hryushka stays focused. He spills one scoop of dog food. He knows one scoop holds roughly thirty-two kibbles. He feels around on the floor, counting as he retrieves them, until he hits thirty-two, then he feels around more, shining the keychain flashlight to where he can't reach. When he's done his father will check the floor carefully. For now, Hryushka doesn't even think about what might be happening on the outside. That is how his father taught him.

Even when he breaks a little padlock and glues two of his fingers together while trying to glue the lock back together he doesn't spaz. He has plenty of time actually, and he sits long after he's done, zippered in the seventh sack with his single scoop of sugar, flour, salt, dog food, buckwheat, and semolina, sucking on his glued-together fingers before rocking himself back and forth against the side of the freezer, signaling to his father that the game is over.

Itchy, this guy in a pickup says to Hryushka.

I don't know what you mean, Hryushka says from the sidewalk, unsure what language the guy is speaking.

Hey, chief, he says. Where's the library?

Oh, Hryushka says. You're right in front of it. It's here.

Then he walks into the library and sits down with the ESL pamphlets. He is trying to rid himself of reflexive particles. He knows he should not feel himself bad. He should feel bad. He should not feel himself like his bones are exploding in the night. He should feel like his bones are exploding in the night. His father never spoke Russian to him, only self-taught English with his thick accent, the same accent that home-schooled him, and now he's the only kid around who doesn't really speak English or Russian, no native language, just a thick accent all his own.

Hryushka heard somewhere that his name means piglet. He feels it but can't directly translate. He feels the pigletness in the sound of his name. He hears things all the time around him, in The Briefcase of the Pregnant Spylady, from the luggage compartment of the Greyhound, he hears them.

Once some grandma, one of the émigrés who used to shop in The Briefcase of the Pregnant Spylady, gave him a Russian language textbook. She felt sorry for him because he couldn't speak what he could understand. His father caught him reading and burnt it in the wood stove.

We not emigrate so you beet Russian, he said. Want that we go anywhere.

When Hryushka hears a word in either language, it's not like he hears the word. It kind of bypasses his ears and an image pops into his head. When he hears his own name a piglet pops into his head.

The Library is across the street from The Briefcase of the Pregnant Spylady and their attached apartment. Now that he's twelve his father lets him go on his own in the mornings to study. There is no need for him in the shop. It used to be the only Russian store in the city. There were always frozen pelmeni to sweep up (the bags break and the pelmeni skid across the restaurant floor like hockey pucks) or farmer's cheese to rotate (the old stuff he opens out back for the pigeons). Now there's two other stores. Even though his father's prices are cheaper, no one comes anymore.

At noon Hryushka walks across the street for lunch. His father has prepared kielbasa and cheese sandwiches and the stereo is blasting *There Is No God*, his father's favorite song, the only song he ever listens to. It's a seventies rock ballad repeating the words—and only the words, *there is no God*. It's in Russian, so Hryushka is not sure how he knows what's being said, he just knows. His father's got a whole tape with that one song taking up both sides. Every day he plays it, over and over, the only pauses the time it takes to walk to the stereo and flip the cassette. His father sings along as he slices deli meats. It's why none of the other émigrés shop here. They're all Orthodox and that kind of thing gets to them. Like definite and indefinite articles, his father doesn't understand.

They eat and Hryushka cleans the store. He feather dusts shelves and boxes of flours and grains and mixes, vinegars the glass on the freezer doors. His father wipes off the cash register keys. Sometimes, an utterance comes out of Hryushka's mouth and he has no idea why he says it. When he is perplexed and agitated sometimes: Horseradish doesn't know! Before they play the game again, his father says, No fur, no feathers, and Hryushka replies, To the devil. He has no idea why.

Hryushka knocks himself against the side of the storage cabinet when he's done. His father lifts him out of the seventh sack and brushes him off with the back of his hand.

How legs? his father asks.

Cramped, Hryushka says. It's hard to turn around.

Not much time, he says. Your body wants grow. His father dumps out the seventh sack and checks the bottom of the storage cabinet. We do a real thing now. Once more.

The real thing, Papa, one more time.

The trick to the prices is logistics. Every two weeks Hryushka and his father take a trip to New York on the Greyhound. When they get there, Hryushka's father rents a van one-way and drives product back, direct from the wholesalers; they pick it up themselves at the warehouses in Brooklyn. It's still expensive but cheaper than dealing with distributors. The other stores have the goods shipped in and poppy seed buns go for two bucks each. The Briefcase of the Pregnant Spylady sells them for one dollar.

The weather broke tonight, a freak cold snap on the heels of a front, rain then ice. On the way to the Greyhound station, Hryushka keeps bending down to pick up bracelets off the sidewalk but they're frozen worms glittering under the street lights. He pockets them and they break like pencil leads in his pocket. Before they reach the station they step into an alley and his father opens up the suitcase, which is insulated with rabbit fur. Hryushka climbs in and his father snaps it shut.

As his father rolls the suitcase across the asphalt, Hryushka loses himself. He forgets where he is, does not turn on the keychain flashlight, closes his eyes as tight as possible so as not to witness all the dark. He thinks how the cold snap came on like his growth spurt, from nowhere, pang to the bone. He shot up three inches this month. He cries in the night, massaging his legs and starving. His father brings him carrots and tells him to think small. He tries to think small. He tries to imagine his legs the size they used to be, but he finds that he has a great deal of trouble picturing his legs without looking at them.

It is easy to tell when his father hands him off. The driver is never as careful with the suitcase. He is dropped, then flipped upside down, then thrown. He hears his father ask the driver to be more careful. The driver gives the suitcase an extra hard shove to the back of the compartment.

This is the part that always seems to take forever, idling at the station. His father watches where his son is positioned in the luggage compartment and tries to sit above him. The bus is full of other émigrés going from Cleveland to Squirrel Hill. His father talks so loud that Hryushka can sometimes hear his sputtering voice over the engine noise.

The real thing is quite a bit different than the game. For one, there is no scoop. The scoop was his father's idea, to get Hryushka to concentrate on process and technique. There are no prearranged bags of granule; instead piles of suitcases, most of them locked at best with a little padlock, which Hryushka can easily pick. The little padlocks his father buys for the game are much higher quality than these.

Other things are similar. He is only to take one thing from each bag, just one thing, his father always said. If you took just one thing, he said, no one notice. He wanted them not to notice as much as possible. If it was just one thing, they could never be sure they hadn't left it, no one could make a case. It should be something valuable, usually jewelry. Sometimes he found cash, a laser pointer, massagers, a prosthetic hand. Another of his father's rules: if there is nothing of value, he still has to take something from each bag for consistency and fairness. Here Hryushka's own rule comes into play: he never takes anything he himself wants. He leaves the candy. Once he happened on a porno collection—he looked, but left it. Instead, from these bags, he takes toenail clippers, Rogaine, and XXL t-shirts, which are too big for him even to sleep in.

The first leg of the trip—mostly Russians—he is to stay put. His father always told him to forget about what's going on outside, to relax, because he can feel by the speed of the bus how fast it's going. If it slows, it's getting off the highway and a stop will come soon. If it slows, he's to climb immediately back into the suitcase. As long as the speed is constant, they're still on the highway and everything's fine. Highway = fine. He should forget about what's going on outside, relax. The first time they pull off the highway—you cannot miss that from the luggage compartment—they will be in Pittsburgh, some bags will be pulled off, others put on, better bags. But there will be plenty of time from that first slowing to Pittsburgh, so he can relax.

Hryushka does not stay put this time. His legs are cramping. There is a special pocket on the top of the suitcase, which looks like a zipper pocket. The zipper is on the inside. He squeezes his skinny body out of the pocket like a stick of chewing gum from its pack. The compartment vibrates and he bangs his head on the steel sheet of flimsy metal separating the luggage from the people.

He turns on the keychain light and looks around. He knows how to spot the good bags, the kind kids his age or a little older pack. They're like sports bags athletes carry. They say *Nike* or *Reebok* or *Fine Young Thing* on the outside. They are never locked. He shines his keychain flashlight on a green one. He pulls up the side of the bag and reads: *Phuket Thailand.* The bus is barreling, maybe seventy-five, eighty.

Ordinarily he would avoid the temptation of a Phuket Thailand bag, but his legs are stretched and better feeling, though he's hungry again. Hryushka can barely remember a time before he had taken this trip in the luggage compartment. It was always there, something he understood but couldn't explain. He tried to remember the first time he'd played the game, but he couldn't remember that either. He might never get the chance to root around in another kid's bag. And this bag—he can't figure out how to pronounce this word. It wouldn't hurt to peek, he figures.

He opens the zipper and crawls in. There is no sound more exciting to him than that of a zipper. Inside, the bag smells of pecan. To him, the flannels and jeans are softer than his father's fur. His head knocks against something hard and flat. He reaches under a stack of undershirts and removes a CD player with headphones, something he's always wanted. He can't understand why the kid wouldn't take the headphones with him to listen on the bus. If Hryushka had headphones and he was riding on the bus with a ticket, he would surely take them with him. Hryushka hits the open/close button.

As the CD player opens, Hryushka hears the squeal-hiss of the bus brakes, then the slow pull as it merges into the exit lane. He removes a length of frozen worm from his pocket and shines the flashlight on it. It's beginning to thaw and come back to life, writhing almost imperceptibly. He places it under the stack of undershirts then climbs out of the Phuket Thailand bag, rezips it, scales the stacks of luggage back to his own suitcase. Still clutching the CD player, he dives back in.

He is sweating and nervous as the brakes—Hryushka

imagines the collective whine of a million beagles—bite then release. He hears the driver pop the luggage compartment door, toss out bags around him, chuck others in. Then, to his shock, his own suitcase and he himself are removed, plopped to the ground briefly then picked up and carried, a circuitous route by very sure steps, distinctly his father's calculated steps. The suitcase is dropped to the ground again, then the latches snapped and the top lifted open.

Hryushka blinks. He is in a stall next to a toilet, his father standing over him, saying, Come out, Hryushka. You have a whole life to ride bus. Might well as start now. His father leaves the stall and washes his hands. Hryushka steps out of the suitcase, sticking the CD player and headphones down his pants. Then they leave the bathroom together.

Hryushka's father buys an additional ticket from the attendant, and Hryushka watches the driver's face as he and his father emerge from the terminal, a place awash in such white a light—Hryushka can hardly imagine having seen a place so bright before. His father hands the driver his stub and Hryushka's ticket. Then he hands over the empty suitcase.

I deposited some things for my wife and picked my son, his father says, motioning toward Hryushka.

Fine, the driver says. He frisbees the suitcase into the compartment. It lands right on top of the Phuket Thailand bag.

Hryushka doesn't understand what's going on, but since he has never ridden in a bus like a normal ticketed person he doesn't worry. He takes the window seat beside his father and absorbs all the silence, amazed at how quiet the bus is from up here. He always thought he heard so much talking, but here there is nothing but the silence of strangers absorbed in their seats. He glances at his father, whose eyes are closed, his head held perfectly straight.

He closes his eyes and briefly imagines himself back inside the Phuket Thailand bag. He looks over the seatbacks for a little boy to go with it. He goes to the bathroom and on his way stares intently at the crooked sleeping heads of the other passengers. No boy. He balances the CD player on the little bus-bathroom faucet. Something occurs to him then as he's peeing: perhaps whoever's bag that was was someone like him, another boy whose father hides him in the luggage to steal what there is to steal. Suppose that little boy snuck out of the bag before Hryushka, and he was investigating another suitcase—maybe even his own—as he stole the kids' CD player. More likely, the kid rode the bus the first leg, then had his accomplice—someone like his own father—install him in the luggage at the same time as Hryushka's father inexplicably let him out. The idea was just outrageous enough. Hryushka had never considered a possibility like this before.

On the way back down the aisle he looks not for people like himself, but for people who look like his father. They pretty much all could be him in one way or another.

Hryushka's father has ordered special pies from the distributors. He is taking the store in this direction, in the direction of desserts. He's specifically ordered Napoleon, Stump, and Kiss of an African Man. He asks the wholesaler in English for his pies, and the guy replies something about credit and then Hryushka's father shoos Hryushka out and he and the wholesaler argue in Russian.

Hryushka and his father leave with no Napoleons, Stumps, or Kisses of African Man. They have a couple boxes of candy Squirrels and frozen chocolate bars filled with farmer's cheese. They rent a Kia rather than the mini-van because they have only a trunkful of product to transport and Hryushka sleeps most of the way across New York when something else strange happens: In a town called Corning above the Finger Lakes, Hryushka's father pulls off the highway and into the parking lot of the Corning Museum of Glass.

The building itself, surprisingly, is brick. But inside everything is glass. Hryushka can see, across the room, a glass Egyptian pharaoh at least four times bigger than himself. His father, for the second time in so many days, hands him a ticket. On this one is written *Corning Museum of Glass: After spending time here you will understand glass in a very different way.*

Hryushka looks down at the ground as he's stocking the candies and chocolate covered farmer's cheese in the reach-in cooler. He gets slightly dizzy then walks over to the mark on the wall his father uses to track his height.

Hryushka presses his back against the wall trim. His father is flipping the tape and restarting *There Is No God.*

Can you measure me, Papa? he says.

His father runs a pencil across the top of Hryushka's head. He steps away from the wall and they both look at it. The new mark is separated from the old one by approximately the height of one poppy seed bun.

His father falls back into a corner, then slides down to a sitting position below a speaker. Both of them stare at the bun-sized space. His father's legs are stretched out in front of him. The only sound, except for the *There Is No God* refrain, is the reach-in cooler fans.

Hryushka wants to ask why he was pulled off the bus in Pittsburgh, but he doesn't. He is thinking about *some* and *any.*

He is not sure when to say *Is there any problem?* or *Is there some problem?* He's not sure what the difference is.

His thoughts are interrupted by his father's voice in Russian, explaining something, though at first Hryushka is not sure what. Then he realizes that he is telling the story of the store's name. Hryushka listens, and it is difficult, but images begin to appear in his head: His father's father used to walk with him through the common wagons on the Russian trains and slip him into the compartments under the seats when people went to the bathrooms. He had to be quick. In those days he wouldn't get much but everything was worth something. He'd be happy if he found half a loaf of bread wadded in a head scarf. But there came a time—as with Hryushka—when he started to grow. Hryushka's father was sad not because he particularly liked stealing from people, but because he liked climbing among their things. On what Hryushka's father's father said would be his last trip in the luggage compartment, he made a fabulous discovery, one that stands to this day as his most exciting moment. Amid a compartment of canvas bags and musty suitcases tied together with rope, he discovered a small shiny black briefcase. The locks on it were difficult to pick, but he had a good knife, and though his father would have killed him if he had found out, he broke the locks to get in. In that briefcase was the most strange combination of items. He first noticed a pistol and a kind of radio, both made by Japanese. There were also stacks of folders containing documents labelled *SECRET.* Underneath them, smushed at the bottom of the briefcase were women's underwear and a pacifier with a piece of ribbon around it, a gift tag that read, *For Mashinka—my favorite pregnant spylady—and offspring.*

Hryushka's father goes on with the story, but Hryushka stops listening. He now has an image in his head of his father as a little kid, hunkered under a seat compartment and fumbling through the belongings of a pregnant KGB agent. He takes that image with him to bed, where he gets under the sheet and toys with the CD player he'd stolen from the Phuket Thailand bag. Inside is a CD with a piece of tape and the word *Rach* written on it. He puts the headphones on and hits play. He'd expected Van Halen or Aerosmith, but it's classical, piano. He lies there listening.

Later he pads down the hall and across the corridor into The Briefcase of the Pregnant Spylady, where his father is still crouched in the corner, his back to the wall, his hands on his knees, mouthing the words to his favorite song.

Let's try one more time, Papa, Hryushka says.

Hryushka's father tells him to take a pillow but he says it like *pilaf*. He can curl around it since he is really too big for the suitcase and with the CD player again shoved down the front of his pants it cushions things. During the hand-off he hears the driver ask his father what the hell he's got in there.

Barbells, his father says. Sorry.

Hryushka relaxes through the idling, until they've pulled out and he knows they're on the freeway by the vibrations of the flimsy sheet metal lining the luggage compartment and the whoosh of air beneath him. Then he slides himself out of the suitcase and shines the flashlight around.

Mostly the usual stuff. He shines the flashlight on an expensive-looking silver luggage set. He climbs toward it but once there his eye catches something back in the corner of the compartment. He points the flashlight and sees the very same Phuket Thailand bag he stole the CD player from. This had never happened before, that he'd encountered the same bag twice.

He climbs over the expensive silver luggage set and punches the Phuket Thailand bag, not knowing exactly what to expect. It does not react. He unzips it and shines the flashlight in. It's packed much like it was before, like it's missing something about the size of a body. He climbs in and pushes his shoulders back into the flannels, extends his legs as far as they'll go. He zips himself in. The bag is longer and stretchier than his father's suitcase.

He takes out the stolen CD player, fits the headphones over his ears, and starts the piano music again, dulling the bus noise to a background buzz. He breathes in the smell of this kid's bag—not nuts exactly, more like the underneath of library desks. He closes his eyes. He grips denim, feels his hands into a small cardboard box. He shakes it and it flutters. Band-Aids, he guesses. He sees only dark and hears only this strange piano music. He puts the box of Band-Aids into his pocket.

It's more comfortable in this bag, Hryushka thinks. I feel all here.

When the Greyhound comes to a full stop—how did he miss the pulling off the highway?—he doesn't hit pause on the CD player. The door on the luggage compartment roars open, annoying him. He's lifted with the Phuket Thailand bag and thrown on the sidewalk.

Hryushka hears people move all around him, picking up other cases that are not him. It seems like he waits forever, for all of the buses to pull away, for someone to give the now seventy-pound heavier Phuket Thailand bag a puzzled tug, and then comes the unzipping.

When the bright bus station lights shine in, Hryushka prepares a big smile for a boy who turns out to look exactly like he expected him to look. They stare into each other's faces, each of them thinking the other is something he is not. Hryushka breaks the silence. A pancake in general, he says.

Owned

THAT'S US, TWO DUDES AND THE GIRL WITH THE iguana down her shirt. You can tell the bartender's a little concerned. Yeah, I would be too. But the iguana's mine. Sylvia is Brian's. We're all on these big red horse tranquilizers that were Sylvia's so in a sense we're all—me, Brian, everyone else in the world, the bartender and the iguana—we're all hers.

The bar is the bartender's. The big screen TV is his and so is the cable. The draft Buds are ours only because we just bought them. Prior to that they were his. I'm not saying anything any normal person don't already know. The palm tree and that planter with all the dirt the palm tree grows out of are the bartender's. The windows that remind me of sunlights because the whole joint reminds me of a greenhouse are his. I'm tired.

The Knicks are mine. The Pacers are Brian's. The iguana is Sylvia's now. It never sits still for me. I don't even know why I brought it, but after we took the pills it seemed like the right thing. It bites me. It sits under her shirt, softly pressing its nails into her white tits. Softly, I'm guessing, because, I'm guessing, it's not breaking the skin or else she's just not saying anything. She's got its neck pressed into the blue vein at the base of her neck. Its tail rides out from underneath her shirt.

I tell her the thing's going to bite. "It's mine," she says.

"You can have it," I tell her.

"I'll pay you," she says. "I'll pay the shit out of you."

"Just buy the next beer," I say.

The bartender is yelling at his customers, the ones that raised certain concerns in quiet tones about the iguana being in the bar. He's yelling for them to get out of his bar and take their quiet concerns with them. "I'm supportive of regular occupants of barstools!" he yells. He's not ready yet to call the barstools ours.

Brian wants his Pacers. He wants his Pacers bad. He didn't know they were playing. He didn't know he'd be watching his Pacers. Now he wants them though. "I love this team, man. I want this team," he's saying.

I lean over and nap. And when I hunch up, Sylvia has the iguana in the planter. It's snapping at her and she's thumping it with her jet-black nails. Brian is able to lift his chin off the bar because the Knicks are ahead. He's forgotten that his were the Pacers. The bartender is curled up in the corner asleep underneath the sinks.

Sylvia takes off her shirt and wraps up the iguana's head in it. She flips it. It flings its tail at her. She spits on it. It hisses.

"Throw me a spoon," she says. I throw her a plastic spoon. She spoons soil on it now.

"How do you have the energy?" I manage.

"It's mine," she says.

James Stories

right thing. It bites me. It sits under her shirt, softly pressing its nails into her white tits. Softly, I'm guessing, because, I'm guessing, it's not breaking the skin or else she's just not saying anything. She's got its neck pressed into the blue vein at the base of her neck. Its tail rides out from underneath her shirt.

I tell her the thing's going to bite. "It's mine," she says.
"You can have it," I tell her.
"I'll pay you," she says. "I'll pay the shit out of you."
"Just buy the next beer," I say.

The bartender is yelling at his customers, the ones that raised certain concerns in quiet tones about the iguana being in the bar. He's yelling for them to get out of his bar and take their quiet concerns with them. "I'm supportive of regular occupants of barstools!" he yells. He's not ready yet to call the barstools ours.

Brian wants his Pacers. He wants his Pacers bad. He didn't know they were playing. He didn't know he'd be watching his Pacers. Now he wants them though. "I love this team, man. I want this team," he's saying.

I lean over and nap. And when I hunch up, Sylvia has the iguana in the planter. It's snapping at her and she's thumping it with her jet-black nails. Brian is able to lift his chin off the bar because the Knicks are ahead. He's forgotten that his were the Pacers. The bartender is curled up in the corner asleep underneath the sinks.

Sylvia takes off her shirt and wraps up the iguana's head in it. She flips it. It flings its tail at her. She spits on it. It hisses.

"Throw me a spoon," she says. I throw her a plastic spoon. She spoons soil on it now.

"How do you have the energy?" I manage.

"It's mine," she says.

James Stories

James's Fear of Birds

I KEPT EPI THROUGH THE WEEKEND. IT WAS MY girlfriend's bird, a wretched thing. I watched it while she cheated on me with some dude in another town. She left every couple of weeks and I kept Epi during these times.

James came over a lot. Birds terrified him. He'd sit on the couch eyeing her, drinking this scotch we drank over ice that we both swore made us hallucinate.

Why are you so scared of birds anyway? I asked James once.

This thing from my childhood, he said.

What happened?

I don't want to talk about it just keep that fucking bird away from me.

This was easier said than done. I kept Epi on the floor. She'd walk up your feet though, trying to get to your shoulder. A cockatiel. A sorry specimen.

I like birds. I mean, I like the idea of being a guy who likes birds. Someone who might watch them as the main activity of a day. That's the kind of thing I like people thinking about me.

But in reality I'm not so good with pets. Like when Epi shits on my shoulder, I crumble her up in my fist and throw her fast pitch into the cushion. Then I immediately feel bad. I pick her up, lovingly this time, rubbing her head. I apologize. I pray that she will not die. I pray genuinely for her sake and not for the sake of my own ass. Then I kind of forget about it. And she nips my earlobe or something and I do the same thing all over.

James likes watching this. He hopes I'll kill her. That's how much he hates birds. He wishes they all were dead.

I wish all birds were dead, he says.

We're well into the scotch that makes us hallucinate.

The thing is James kind of looks like a bird. He has this huge nose. You can't help but think: beak.

About 3 a.m. I call my girlfriend's apartment and some dude answers.

Hello, he says.

Who is this? I say.

Who is this? he says.

Who is it? James says.

Shhh, I say. Look, as far as I know you're not supposed to be there.

Eff off. Mina said I should meet her here tonight. She gave me a key.

How do I know you're not robbing the place?

Come on over, he says. I'll kick your ass.

Naw, I say.

What are you? Her boyfriend?

She said she wasn't coming in until tomorrow.

She's meeting me here in the morning, man. Is that going to be okay with you?

Well, I still don't know you're not robbing the place.

Why would I pick up the phone if I was a robber, you dumb eff?

Get him to tell you something only she would know, James says.

Tell me something only she would know, I say. It's kind of embarrassing to be doing this in front of James.

If only she knows it, how do I know?

You know what I mean. There's two of us, we'll come over there. We'll call the cops.

I said come on over. What do you want anyway? I met her last week in the tampon aisle. Big Bear. We've been doing it ever since.

All right, I say. It's probably true anyway. True enough.

Bye, I say.

Bye, he says.

Epi shits on my shoulder during the call. I feel the spot of heat, but don't thump her off.

Well. You already knew she was cheating on you, James says.

Yeah but.

Wait a second, he says. You knew he was there, didn't you? Why'd you call if you thought she was out of town?

I don't know. Answering machine. I wanted to talk into her answering machine.

We sit for a while. Sit very still. Then Epi hops across the floor towards James's feet—the James on-ramp. I intercept her.

We need to kill that bird, he says.

We're not killing the bird.

We need to kill that bird.

Couldn't I just spray paint WHORE on her door or something?

That's doable, James says, down the line.

I live in a pink house and not many people drive down my street. Epi hops off my finger and stands there like an idiot. In the street. She has no idea.

I'm not really into this, I say.

It has to be done.

I pull off my Puma and half-heartedly wing it at her. She hops out of the way and stands there again, watching us. Then she hops toward us. She doesn't want to waste any of her precious shit on the ground when she could drop it on one of us.

That's not going to cut it, James says.

He removes a hammer from his back pocket.

Where'd you get that?

Earlier, he says.

Epi is nearly upon him. He trembles slightly then punts her back out into the street. He follows, brings the hammer down on her square. Her body explodes. But James doesn't stop there. He pounds again and again and again until she is a bloody nothing.

He throws the hammer into the flower bed and we sit down to smoke. We smoke.

This is not right, I say.

We sit there a while not looking at the street.

You want me to tell you why I'm scared of birds? he says. It's simple, really.

Here, there is a pause.

A duck's quack doesn't echo, he says.

Every sound echoes, I say.

Not a duck's quack. We had one once at the Grand Canyon.

You brought a duck to the Grand Canyon?

We found one there. As you said, everything around echoed, voices, our footsteps, whistling. But when that duck opened its beak, nada. It bit too.

Then Epi appears on his foot. He loses it. I mean he really goes out of control at this. I am shocked, but composed.

I reach down and she hops onto my finger. She sits there long enough for me to examine her. Clean. No damage. She scales my arm.

Not again, James repeats over and over.

We better get inside, I say.

And this is the weirdest thing. As soon as we step through the door, she flies. She flies, man. All around the room, seven, eight, ten times. This bird has never flown in its life.

So James and I, after this, are pretty confident we're just sharing a vision. And we kind of get into it.

Epi flies these circles of varying width. A dropping appears on the top of my foot as if out of nowhere. I left the Puma somewhere in the street and I don't care. Then at the completion of one circle she goes right for James, lighting on his shoulder. He'd be freaked out normally, if just a normal hallucinatory bird landed on his shoulder. But this is a hallucinatory bird that he just hammered into the pavement, so he's petrified.

And there, after a moment, Epi transmogrifies into my girlfriend. My girlfriend sits there on his shoulder, and she watches me. But I can't be sure we're sharing the vision anymore, so, to calm him, I say, Go with it. This is all a hallucination, man. That bird is dead in the street.

I know, he says, all of a sudden I just feel completely deflowered.

Which is good, for him.

The Back of the Line

As I turn into the driveway, a turn I know by memory, I don't even look up. I run into the back of a man. The top of my head contacts him first, then the rest of me.

My bad, I say.

He gives me a little shove with a clipboard. Watch it, he says, and hands me a pencil, which I fumble and drop.

There's a commotion, I see, now. A line of men from the door of the house all the way up the driveway to the sidewalk, where I am, at the back. All the men are filling out forms on clipboards with pencils. Cars stop in the street, pause, then back up to the curb. Men get out of the cars and fall into line behind me. Clipboards and pencils are passed back. There's been an investment made on someone's part in clipboards and pencils.

An application is clipped to each clipboard, your standard job app with some questions whited out and new ones penned in. It's been through several rounds of photocopy.

Another car stops in the street. The driver points at the window of the house. Him and his passenger both squint, then the car backs on up to the curb. I have to step out of line to see what he was pointing at: A sign taped to the inside of the window next to the door, *Boyfriend Wanted: Apply Within.* The text is written in black marker, Sharpie, her unmistakable hand, on poster board. It's written big so you make no mistake from the street.

She wastes little time.

I rejoin the line but the guy who was behind me, who I'd just handed a clipboard and pencil in a friendly noncompetitive way, won't let me back in. He jerks his head. The guys behind him look up from their applications to give me the fuck-you eyes. I've never been good at lines. I go to the back.

I start filling out the basic information, and, as others get in line behind me, I play along, passing the clipboards and pencils back, a little less friendly now, a little more competitive.

I'm glad she thought to give pencils rather than pens because I'm not so good at filling out forms either and keep messing up. I write above the lines when I should be writing below them, my last name where my first should be, my city for my street address. I erase all over. I write *n/a* in a lot but at least I know to never leave a blank blank. Either write *n/a* or *none.* Like where it says *Characterize your appetite for satisfaction. Use the back of this application if you need more space.* I write *n/a* there. Where it says *Your approximate annual income?* I write *none.*

As I'm erasing and mostly n/a-ing, I glance at the faces of those leaving the house. Some were invited inside for a moment, some leave after passing off their clipboards and mumbling thanks. You can tell a lot by just looking. I know the looks. I've gotten and not gotten many positions. To those beaten, pale, I nod my head and bite my lower lip. To those with a little spring in their step, I jut my chest out and try to look bad.

Then James comes out wearing a t-shirt that says, *Must Be This Tall to Ride.*

James, I say, James, man.

I leer, he says.

I know that.

Some friend. He knows, he says to the sky, or to Jesus I guess. I'm at the bus stop yesterday thinking I'm casually giving this chick the eye when she snaps, he says. Starts screaming at me right there. "You numb pig. Why you leer at me? You're no man." I said, "Whoa. I hadn't intended to leer." She called me out, man. And you knew.

You look a little too long is all.

There's a lot of things I never wanted to be that I've been, but I really never wanted to be that. Never.

Meanwhile the line moves forward and I move forward with it. James walks backward to keep up with me.

So I'm heading home with this self-loathing, this label, and thinking what I need to cure myself is a girlfriend. A real genuine girlfriend. One I can look at. Then I see this sign. He points over his shoulder to the poster board. Serenity.

You remember she's *my* old girlfriend right?

Yeah, but she cheated on you all the time.

Still, I say.

It's worth applying for, you know. It's free.

I walk in place in line to get my shoelaces vibrating and distract me from these tools. I'm in this habit of watching my shoelaces. They vibrate when my feet hit the sidewalk. It keeps my mind off her. When it's my turn I keep going up the steps watching the shoelace vibrations until the top of my head hits her, just like it did the guy at the back of the line, letting me know I'm there.

She looks not pleased to see me.

How many goddamn clipboards and pencils did you buy for this? I say without meaning to.

You've got to be prepared just as much for success in your endeavors, my love, she says, as you are for failure.

So what are your qualifications? She snatches the clipboard and looks over it. This is not the free lunch line.

I'm of average height, I say. I drink but don't smoke. My feet are soft due to daily cocoa butter application. I miss somebody.

It's smudgy, she says.

I'm better with spray paint, I say.

I have a couple weeder questions. What's the most interesting thing you could think of to do with this?

She produces a pork chop bone.

I fondle it, long since dried and sharp, like fish teeth. Slingshot, I say.

She jots something down on my application, in the space where it says *Do not write here. For office use only.* I broke up with you for a reason: You're only the fourth motherfucker to give such an obvious answer today.

I sense I am not doing well and ask to use the bathroom.

Step inside, she says. I'm only giving you fair shake because I believe in equal opportunity for all scumbags.

Which I appreciate about her. In there, I take a little extra time. I never really thought I'd make it back. Sure, it used to be when we were broken up, well, once at least, she called me up and said, Do you think you can get hard? But those were different times. I breathe deep the smell of Anti-Bacterial Country Apple Hand Gel, which is, for me, the smell of her.

When I come out I say, You love scumbags.

But I want the best scumbag, she says, and hands me a plastic slingshot, the kids' kind. And this? The most interesting thing? she says.

Pork chop bone, I say.

Okay, she says, nodding, holding eye contact now. Better.

She points me toward the couch. She stands and reexamines my application. You find a number of my queries don't apply to you.

This is some production, I say. What did James think to do with the pork chop?

All applicant information, she says, is strictly confidential. She's always been like this. Everything is official and efficient with her. And that kind of thing won't get you the position, already a staggering improbability.

I'm just saying, I say.

If you must know, he had a very right answer, she says. As for me, I've decided I want a scumbag who can do math.

Okay. Math.

So. Here. You get to come back in the morning.

What she puts in my hands now is a two-page, double-sided math test. It's a photocopy of the test that Subway gives its prospective sandwich artists. I think I have one of these at home. She's attempted to Sharpie out the Subway logo at the top but you can still see. It's stapled in the top right-hand corner. And a pink appointment slip for tomorrow.

I walk out thumbing through the Subway math test. It's mostly multiplication and division. There is some algebra on the back of the last page where your job is to tell what X is.

Me, James is saying to this one guy when I walk into the Laundromat Bar, and nodding his head a lot. He's at a table with four other guys, all of them from the line. They're hunched over their Subway tests. There's a calculator in the middle of the table.

How long you been here? I ask to be polite.

Long, James says.

I walked for hours, I say, trying to seem not annoyed. I picked up my laundry. I came here to wash. But pretty soon I'm drinking and forgetting that my clothes are in the washer. We pass the calculator around the table. I do the multiplication on the calculator then work out the long division on bar napkins. It says to show your work, but I have to practice it a couple times before I'm ready to show it. James's tongue touches his nose when he writes. He shields his eyes whenever a woman falls into his line of sight. I see him peeking through the fingers though.

I don't say a word for a long time and James finally calls me out.

Why are you taking this so seriously? he asks.

I'm trying to get things right this time.

Maybe the gig isn't for you.

It's for you then? Or one of them tools? One of the tools blows up at this and James tells him he can sit the fuck back down. The tool listens to James. People tend to.

I'm looking out for my buddy, and you never make callbacks.

You leer, I say to James.

The new bartender gives last call.

And I'm doing something about that. No thanks to you, he says and makes for the Galaga machine. He always gets on Galaga at last call because he can play forever. The old bartender knew to cut it off before last call.

With his back to me, I switch out James's test with my own. Then I get up and leave.

In my pink home, I hunker down. All the lights off. I

lock the doors and try the old creaky futon. James shows up several hours later, ramming parts of himself at the door. Chunks of asphalt shatter the window and land on the futon beside me. He's screaming something but all I can make out is *wooden* and *ordinary*.

I take my pillow and the math test and crawl around the glass and back to the bathroom, shutting and bolting the bathroom door, then arranging myself on the floor around the toilet. With my elbow on the pillow it's actually nice. I may come here again. And the door muffles James just enough so that his ranting is background noise, like running water or a good ceiling fan or central air conditioning, which always comforts me at night.

I flip through his math test. There's ornate, intricate Xs through every question. Different designs and shapes make up the lines of the Xs, flowers, tribal, bubbles, little Galaga ships, and some horned demon Xs. It's the kind of doodling he does above the urinals at the Laundromat Bar. Things made up of other things. There's a bar napkin attached with a paperclip. I wonder where he got a paperclip. The napkin is blank except for the fragrance of Old Milwaukee and an equation:

$$\frac{\text{Appetite for Satisfaction}}{\text{Desire}} - \text{Demand for Love}$$

James continues his tantrum in the street. I am curled up on the bathroom floor reading over this thing and having no idea what it means, an enormous feeling of inadequacy washing over me.

I remember then leaving my clothes in the washer at the Laundromat Bar. By the time I show up tomorrow there will have been ashtrays and pints of beer poured over them, and, not having enough quarters to rewash, I'll simply dry them. Instead of appearing at my appointment for the boyfriend position, I'll be sitting there watching flecks of cigarette ash appear in the fog of the dryer glass.

James was right. I never make callbacks. Whenever I apply for a position, for any position, it's not enough that I *showed up*, that I filled out their application, that I talk to them face-to-face. They always want something more of me. No. I have to go do something, and it's either a math test or a reference or piss in a cup or some other meaningless thing I'll fuck up. It's always I never had a chance.

James's Low Moment

JAMES LAY ON THE CHEESE MOLDY CARPET IN HIS
new basement apartment watching the centipedes drop out of
the cinderblock north and west walls. Drawers were built into
the panel board east wall, and a bat squirmed out of the built-
in drawer he was using for his underwear. He watched the bat
dive-bomb moths at the light bulb.

He stood up and went to the bathroom where he
discovered an eau de toilette in the medicine cabinet called
One Man Show, which smelled like noodles. He sprayed the
centipedes on the carpet, and it seemed to kill them. They
curled when they died. He picked up the dead centipedes, and
their legs caught in the cheese moldy carpet. He dropped them
in the toilet. He sprayed the One Man Show on the holes in
the cinder block and then he bathed himself in it.

He opened the blinds. The bat smacked into his
underwear drawer trying to get away from the light. It

surprised James that the thing didn't knock itself out. Outside his window, just a few feet from him, there were about fifteen small, old grave markers. It looked like a little family cemetery plot.

James decided to smoke some weed, which he didn't do often because it made him paranoid, but he figured he couldn't be more paranoid than he already was with bats and centipedes and dead bodies a few feet away.

James safety-pinned holes into an old Mountain Dew can and shaped it into a bowl. When the bat hooked its wing-hands in the drawer crevice and wormed in, grunting and peeping in a way James didn't know bats grunted and peeped, he rightfully understood wing-hands for the first time. Then it disappeared, wriggling into a space he doubted would fit mail. He could hear it shuffling around in his underwear, a sound like long blows on cardboard.

This was Sayonara weed, the last present from his ex-girlfriend, who he'd been living with the past three months. It was her parents' house and it felt like a parents' house, a proper home with atmospheric controls, tight sealants on every portal so creatures like centipedes and bats couldn't get in, windows looking out on a yard without a half-ass cemetery. He'd be there right now, breathing the fabric softener in the non-damp sheets and pillowcases rather than cheese mold. He'd be next to her.

The night prior to his eviction a man had entered the parental bedroom, stopped in front of James's girlfriend's mother, opened his fly, and urinated on her head. The parents were awake but claimed they were too mortified to move. The man zipped up and calmly left the bedroom, shutting the door behind him. The parents called the police quietly from the bedside phone. The father dabbed the mother's head with his pillow but she made him stop to preserve DNA. The Rottweilers went ballistic when the police arrived. His girlfriend was woken up too then, but James slept.

The police found no signs of forced entry. They said, Folks, weren't the dogs barking when the intruder came in?

Huh, the parents said, now that you mention that, it's kind of funny. No.

The police asked, Are you certain there's no one else in the house?

James had problems in sleep before, had been found one night sitting up in bed, eyes open, picking at flowers on the sheets and requesting that his girlfriend help him get all these bugs, which caused her to be extremely weirded-out.

The parents looked at their daughter. She pushed open the door and the police flashlights fell on James's face as he slept. Now that they mentioned it, she remembered him going to the bathroom not long before they arrived.

James presented himself at breakfast the next morning, and the mother was there to greet him wearing a nightgown he hadn't seen before.

Good morning, James, she said, over-chipper. Do you recall urinating on my head last night?

He paused to make sure he'd heard correctly. Negatory, he said and reached for a waffle.

Sure was a hoot, she said.

His things, his girlfriend said, were already packed in large Heftys by the curb, but unfortunately it had been Yard Trash Day and the men had picked up. His girlfriend walked with him and explained the fallout.

Out of the kindness of their souls they decided not to press charges, she said, on the contingency that you leave.

Can you claim kindness of the soul when there's a contingency? he asked.

She was calm about the whole thing. Actually, she said, they've been looking for an excuse to bon voyage you for a while.

And you? You're looking for an excuse to bon voyage me?

Here's some weed, she said.

Then she pointed to the depressions in the plush grass where the Heftys containing his things were before the men picked them up.

James didn't think these things were right: kindness of souls, contingencies, excuses, all his worldly possessions mistaken for leaves. Shouldn't there be circumstantial proof *other* than the absence of dogs barking? James had spent time with those dogs, and they'd been known not to bark for reasons other than the person who peed on his girlfriend's mother was him.

James hadn't anticipated what high-quality shit this was. He lay on the floor again. When he lay on the floor of his basement apartment, he realized, he was about exactly six feet under. If he could look through the cinder block with X-ray vision, he would see the bodies or the coffins if the people in the little family cemetery were buried in coffins. They'd be right there.

Down the hall some crazy was beating on a door. It was violent-loud, like it was his own door. Seen you, fuck, the crazy said. Know you there. James put his ear to his own door and it rattled against his head. It *was* his own door. He moved away, sat down by the drawer where the bat and his underwear lived. Uniroyal Tiger Paw Freedoms, the guy said, pounding. Uniroyal Tiger Paw Freedoms.

James stood when the hinge screws groaned. He turned the lock and the door flew open. This hand took him by the ear and pulled him down the hallway and out the door and into the parking lot, where he got his first look at the guy. He laughed out loud the guy looked so much like Mr. Kleen. Mr. Kleen slapped him on the back of the head and pointed at the slashed tires on a red pickup truck, some Chevy.

That funny, Jack? the guy said.

James, James says.

A police car rolled into the parking lot with its lights going but no sirens. James fingered his ear, thinking maybe he was just not hearing them. The ear seemed to be working. He turned to go back to his apartment, and Mr. Kleen took him by the neck.

Here he is officer, the guy I called you about, Mr. Kleen said. Fucker cut my tires. I caught him. He squeezed James's neck and released him.

You hauled me out of my apartment, James said.

I saw you duck away, slink like a low moment through the back door. Should've run t'uther apartment, not your own.

I haven't left my apartment in forty hours.

You look distressed, sir, the cop said to me. Are you distressed?

I'm having a crisis, yes, James said, but it does not involve slashing this man's tires. That is not the kind of blip I need on my problem-radar right now. Yet it's fair to count me distressed, I'd agree with that statement, sir. There are other blips.

James wondered if this was one of the cops who shined a flashlight in his sleeping face after the peeing. If so, it couldn't be good. They might try and say he'd slashed the tires in his sleep. He could be blamed for everything from here on out that occurred during a period of time in which it was believed he slept.

The cop squatted to look at the tires and both his knees popped. He ran the back of his knuckle along the frayed rubber.

What'd you call these? the cop said.

Uniroyal Tiger Paw Freedoms, the guy said. One day young.

They good or something?

It's shabbier.

The cop pushed James into the truck, kicked his legs apart, then pulled his right hand behind his back.

My apartment is 10D, James said. I've been in my apartment for at least two days with a number of creatures I'm uncomfortable with. I have nothing, not even a sharp cutting instrument. Except I have some One Man Show cologne that I found in the apartment when I moved in, a couple Mountain Dew. That's it. Maybe a safety pin, drawers.

The cop pulled James's other hand behind his back. James thought he was giving him a hand massage, that it felt rather good, human touch, even a kind like this. He was amazed how relaxed he was, almost asleep.

The cop let him go. Nope, the cop said. That's not your man.

I seen him, the guy says. Seen him golem away.

Can't be. His hands are dirty, in bad need of washing, probably for some time. But no tire marks. See. The cop turns his own hands over and shows us his black knuckles. I just barely touched and you see what they did to me. That's a sign of maybe you didn't get what you paid for. Now were his hands freshly washed, a character like this, we'd had something. I'll take a report, but that's not your man.

The cop went back to his cruiser and sat down in the air conditioning.

It's all right, the guy said. I'm living right next door to you, fool. I'm zeroed-in to every whimper you whimp.

Do you have those drawers in your walls? James asked.

Watch the mouth.

James shut up, but he couldn't really understand it. How was it possible that the walls separating their apartments were thick as drawers? And if they were, were they as thick as two drawers so that the guy had drawers in his apartment too? Did the backs of their drawers bump together? Did they share bats? Because it was one thing a bat crawling through his own underwear, but through his and Mr. Kleen's, that colored the situation.

Mr. Kleen signed a couple forms and then James signed one. Mr. Kleen's name was Ezekiel Rubottom. The statement stated that James had been questioned in connection with the slashing of Ezekiel Rubottom's truck tires, four Uniroyal Tiger Paw Freedoms, which the cop had characterized as *some Pepboys brand*. Ezekiel Rubottom tried to argue with that, but the cop refused to adjust. James should not leave the county.

Back inside his apartment, James tore his copy of the police report into shreds, which he chewed into spitballs and tucked in the cinder block pores of the north and west walls. He kicked the underwear drawer all the way shut, moved the kitchen table against it. He found a centipede scaling his ankle and flicked it off. He reapplied the One Man Show. He crawled under the table and listened at the drawer. No sound. He knocked. Hollow. Nothing.

James's only light bulb blows. He tries to steal one from the hall but the glass covers are bolted on. He thinks about how he could smash the glass without breaking the light bulb inside when he notices two girls standing in an open doorway watching him. There's music coming from the room and the girls are drinking beer.

He waves, and they hold up their beers in his direction, and that is all James needs.

You ladies partying? he says.

Getting there, one of them says.

My girlfriend left me and all I got was this weed, he says, fishing out the film canister from his pocket. James looks into the apartment, where there's six or so people hanging out. He notices a lamp on the table with a light bulb in easy reach.

What was her name? the one says.

Who? James says.

Your girlfriend.

Mattress.

Mattress? they say.

Like box spring? the one girl.

Something other. It was her middle name. I can't say any of them though. She was Hungarian.

I wouldn't like that, she says.

What to expect, James says.

One of the girls smiles. He figures that will be the one he tries to make. She has long black hair and a plastic blue skirt.

Fire it up, this one says to him.

Hold on, he says. He goes back to his apartment and gets the Mountain Dew can. When he returns the girls are gone from the doorway, but the door's still open and he goes in. It's the exact same layout as his minus the panel board wall and the accompanying drawers. Here, cinderblock all around. He puts his ear flush to the west wall and knocks on the cinder block.

He nods to some people and heads for the kitchen where he hears the girls.

A guy turns the corner and holds up a high-five.

Budrow, he says. Who you?

New neighbor, 10D, James says, mind if I drop something on you?

Long as it ain't heavy, Budrow, the guy says.

James changes his line of questioning mid-thought. He decides he doesn't want to think about drawers in walls anymore today. The whole idea of it starts to remind him of Chinese tunnels in Mexicali which he heard about on TV in Mattress's parents' house. He also doesn't want to consider further the idea of one bat, the idea that the bat that lives in his underwear is the sole bat. Much easier to imagine—what do you say, flocks?—of bats in between the walls, but then there'd be more than one showing up in his underwear drawer. He could deal with a flock of bats much easier than with one.

Instead James summarizes the recent ouster from Mattress's parents' place.

I was stone cold when they shined the flashlight in my face—can I get a brew off you?—and they declared me the guy, he says.

Out of control, hombre, Budrow says. Out of control.

James looks around Budrow at the girls who are passing a whiskey bottle between them. The plastic skirt of the one reminds him of a water hose.

Wouldn't it be cooler in here without the lights? James says and pulls the switch on the little table lamp.

Wait a minute, Budrow says. I'm not sure you have anything even to worry about, dogbrother. I'm not exactly sure a crime was committed there. Unless it's a crime to miss the bathroom.

A solid point, James says. Don't they do that for jellyfish stings?

If you were dreaming her head was sucked on by a jellyfish, and let's face it, everyone accepts that we can at least argue the nature of dream-reality versus wake-reality, your move could be considered heroic. Some mothers might say, courageous.

Budrow puts his hand on James's shoulder and pushes

off, walking through the little crowd to the closet, where a couple people have crouched down under some coats because the room is filling up. Definitely not a crime, he says, turning back and shooting James double finger-guns.

James senses that this is already the second time tonight people have slinked away from him. He knows this, and it bums him out but he doesn't want to leave the party without the light bulb. So he takes position at the table in the corner of the kitchen and fires up his Mountain Dew can.

James offers the girls the can. The one he plans to make takes it from him and passes the whiskey.

You live here? James asks.

They nod. We've got a double, they say.

I'm scared to go home, he says. But I'm trying to think of something other than that.

The girls suppose that this is the beginning of James trying to come home with them. They hand him back the weed and reclaim the whiskey and then ignore him. They debate the taste stamina of dried versus liquid bouillon in chili. James leans against the table and unscrews the warm light bulb from the table lamp and puts it in his shorts pocket.

Then Ezekiel Rubottom, his head reflecting the hallway light, appears in the kitchen and wraps both girls' faces up in his armpits. He didn't notice James in the dark.

My chickee babes, he says.

The girls say they've been waiting for him. They say they're going skinny dipping in the creek out back later. He should join them. He says he might, but he might not. They rub his bald head. James didn't know there was a creek out back.

James goes back to his apartment. He screws the stolen light bulb into his fixture and lies down on the cheese moldy rug. The bat is not out and nothing is dropping out of the plugged-up holes in the cinder block. The room seems absent of movement for the first time. He stares at the cinder block wall on the graveyard side. He makes sure his head is lined up with the crosses and puts his arms at his side then he thinks he heard somewhere that you bury people with their feet to the gravestone and does a one-eighty.

A little while later he hears a puffing sound and sees what looks to be a mitten growing out of his underwear drawer. And then, two pair of skinny legs cross his window. He leaps up and sees the girls going around the side of the building.

Just two pair, which means no Mr. Kleen.

James knows it could be bad news if he shows up, but he decides to chance it. He turns off his new light bulb and douses himself with some more One Man Show. He winds around the building past his own window and graveyard and into the back.

There it's a whole other thing. There's a creek wide as an avenue, some lily pads but other than that the water is crystal clear with a smooth rock bottom. He hears some giggling and his eyes follow the creek to a little waterfall, which he cannot believe. He gets a view of the graveyard, sleeps alongside dead bodies, and the folks out the back watch a waterfall draped in kudzu and morning glories. Underneath, a perfect little ledge and two naked girls.

They can't see him yet because he is still in the shadow of the building, but in front of him is a little clearing where the moon shines like a spotlight. He knows he needs a bold move here. He steps into the clearing. He drops his shorts but has to bend over to get out of his underwear.

James was never comfortable with his nakedness, and he plans to get himself in the water straightaway. But the night plays tricks on you. He expects to sink up to his waist, walks high-kneed. He steps in and finds the water and that smooth rock bottom only about ankle deep, the moon bright on him.

He steps again and again, his big toe probing for the drop-off. If anything, it shallows. And once in the middle he sees clearly this is a creek in the true sense of the word. He doesn't know what to do, hadn't quite prepared himself to approach them at this level. He catches the glint off their whiskey bottle and keeps his eyes on the water so maybe they'll think he's hunting metal or crawfish.

The girls see him but they can't tell who he is. By his hair they know not Rubottom. They guess maybe it's their fat neighbor from the second floor.

James turns so he's sideways to them, then reconsiders and turns with his back. Stuck there, his courage drains away. He can't move forward or backward. He stands like that until a bald head shining like the moon rounds the corner, and James thinks, All that is left of my glory.

James's Love of Laundromats

WHAT I AM SUPPOSED TO BE DOING IS TAKING James to the bank and having him sign an Affidavit of Responsibility for the three thou in phone-sex bills he charged up on my girlfriend's phone. She wants no more dealings with him so it falls to me, his best friend. The Affidavit of Responsibility is something that can clear her credit if James doesn't pay up. James is supposed to be paying up, but he doesn't appear to be doing that.

What he appears to be doing is test-driving mopeds. He appears to be sweet-talking the sales guy, and when we get the keys to two spanking new Vespas we appear to be going around the block when what we are doing is stealing them and cruising the streets in search of a new Laundromat.

Our old Laundromat, run by our friend Rodney with hands like pinchers, had gone out of business. The concept had failed. I never liked that combo Laundromat/bar anyway.

Drunk people were always dropping their socks.

We leave downtown and enter the 'villes. James has something very specific in mind. We know we have about thirty minutes tops before the moped people catch on. Near the dry part of town, between Clintonville and Woodville, he cuts me off, swerving into the parking lot of a little strip mall with a Korean grocery and a Battery-Mart. We cruise into the back and roll the mopeds down an embankment into some sewer run off. Then we double back.

What is it? I say.

A potential, he says.

Shouldn't we hit the bank? I say.

We'll do it later, today's our only day off.

We only work half days, but half days turn into whole days when James is around. Next to the Battery-Mart is a dark window that says Cowtown Herps, and I go in there while James checks out the Laundromat.

It smells like moss. A hippie girl is changing a millipede's litter. Little alligators are stacked in black tubs, their mouths electrical-taped.

You've heard of the snakehead? I ask.

I've heard, she says.

Happened to have one?

No, sir. That's an illegal fish.

That's a legal alligator?

Want to see his papers?

An alligator's got papers?

Everything's got papers.

That's a shame, I say.

Wait a sec, she says. You know anything about a snakehead?

I know they can walk.

Walk?

Yeah, walk.

She goes over to a tank and reaches her arm in to the shoulder, wetting her sleeve. She takes an embryo-looking fish out by the head. She drops it on the linoleum where it flops around.

You call that walk? she says.

It's got flounder skin, I say.

It has the motion of walk, back and forth, one side then the other on these flimsy front fins. It basically turns a circle.

He's cute now, but within the year, he'll outgrow that tank. If you sit where he can see you a lot, he'll love you.

Thanks, I say.

When I walk out I hear the ploosh of the snakehead returned to the tank.

The Laundromat is wide and empty except for the most sterling steel washing and drying equipment. Everything new under fluorescent lights. The Laundromat/Bar had hundred-year-old gunk, beige machines tinted purple by lint. The smell of onions about the place. The dryers here exhale, I would say. The washers—petite toploaders to super industrials, which, a sign claims, can take up to sixteen sheets at one time.

The only thing old is the sound system, like spaghetti strainers installed in the ceiling. The sound comes out with a hiss: *In just five weeks, you too can conquer death. Order now to try our program free, and you'll soon be death free.*

James has his arm around a small Korean man, who is smiling.

I've got a million ideas for you, Steve, James says. Euphotopia.

Wednesdays, we're gate-check squad. There are 69 functioning gate arms on campus, which spans less than four square miles. We check each one. We drive a golf cart with a pickup bed. When we find a broken one, and there can be many, especially after football, we have two options: 1) If it snapped close to the mechanism (Reattachment Acceptable), we saw off the splintered end and salvage it. It will still obstruct most of the roadway. 2) If it's broken anywhere near the middle, we chunk it in the Unusable Crate and bolt on a new one.

We make them over by the bus facility because Immediate Supervisor, whose name is Rectifor but who we call Immediate Supervisor, says they cost $200 each from gate arm companies and it's only $20 per with me and James slapping them together. We cut them out of soft pine and attach bendable Plexiglass pieces on the end like Immediate Supervisor wants. James saws the Unusables into shelves for his locker.

I am frustrated with our job and it has a lot to do with the following essential truth: gate arms are not designed to stop anything. You can crack them by looking at them funny. I'm like, if we're going to make gate arms, why don't we *make* gate arms? Something that will really stop somebody or damage some paint? What's the purpose? And for what purpose are we replacing them all the time if they have no purpose?

The only time we see Immediate Supervisor is when we're handing in the Gate Arm Status Report sheets. Other than that, everyone pretty much leaves us alone there, which isn't exactly what we want, since we're going for full-time.

James has the broken gate arm radar. Out of the 69 he can take us direct to the broken ones. Today he is glazy, distant, but still he zeros in on the broken gate arms, and at his direction we hit the West Stadium side first.

Do you know why I love Laundromats? James says, as I am sawing off a splintered end. We sit on the grass to do this and the business of the day—buses, shuttle, bikes, skateboards, cars with permits and cars without—goes by unimpeded.

Why do these gate arms even exist? I say.

Because they're warm. The sound of dryers is a lullaby. If you go into a high-end one, that smell, all Snuggles. You can play video games, eat gumballs, and get change for free. How could it be even more warm, more cozy, more wonderful? Imagine a Laundromat that allows you to snooze, near-naked in an MRI-like tube of fluorescent bulbs, which cook your body while its compatriot machines wash and then heat your clothes to a toasty warm. Warmth in *totale*.

I understand it is about the impression of obstruction, but I can't help feel even more useless than when I didn't have a job, always replacing them when they fail to perform the function they are designed to fail to perform, I say.

I have proposed—and Steve has accepted my proposal—that he incorporate into his Laundromat a tanning facility. Whereas most salons sell thirty-minute or hour-long, Steve's Korean Laundry & Tan's increments will be associated with your wash cycle. At mid-tan you walk out, transfer your clothes, re-up your dryer time and back to tan based on that particular dryer increment.

Forcefields, I say. Forcefields are the future of vehicle-access control. Not these toothpicks. I crack the remains of an Unusable over my knee.

I have a feeling there's some serious work for us over by Research Library, he says.

We pack up and watch one of our new gate arms raise for a Fritos truck.

Immediate Supervisor comes on the walkie-talkie.

Immediate Supervisor, I say. And just then my Nokia buzzes. It's my girlfriend. I drive the cart with my knee and listen to the walkie-talkie with my right ear, the Nokia with my left.

What are you doing after work? my girlfriend says.

Where are you? Immediate Supervisor says.

We're test-driving mopeds, I say to her. We're right here, I say to him.

I cheated on you again last night, she says.

Where's here? Immediate Supervisor says.

His gate arm bigger than mine? I say.

Oh, honey, she says, like tossing a hotdog down a hallway.

Wherever you are, Immediate Supervisor says, get you and your wacko guy over to Research Library. Someone battering-rammed it.

James and I hear the sound of urethane on asphalt. We turn our heads in time to see a rollerblader snap through a gate arm we'd just replaced and speed away down the hill.

James and Steve unpack the tanning bed and I go visit the Herp girl. Maybe it's the ease with which she handles things that bite. I cringe to reach for a teddy bear hamster. She has no fear.

Can we try the snakehead in mud? I say. My feeling is it can walk in mud. We can clear the alligators out of one of these tubs and pack it with mud, then that thing will go.

What snakehead? she says.

The one you threw on the floor the other day.

That wasn't a snakehead. That was a particular catfish which happens to resemble a snakehead. Like I said, snakehead's not legal.

We are standing across from each other, separated by the small cages of the millipedes and tarantulas.

But even if it was a snakehead, she says, which it's not, it couldn't walk in mud. It's a myth, that they walk from lake to lake decimating populations. Thing's got bad press. Might be legal if it weren't for that kind of dis. They decimate populations, sure, eat everything with gills, sure, some amphibians, sure, but they, meaning snakeheads, which is not what is over in that tank in this licensed pet shop subject to wildlife laws and regulations of this fine state, do not walk, period.

She leans across the counter, resting her breasts on a tarantula cage. The tarantula tries to attack them through the aerated lid. It hops at her breasts, but she doesn't seem to care. She sniffs my shoulder.

You have the essence of broth, she says. After the boil. I can smell you coming a mile off.

I eat a lot of soups, I say.

The Laundromat is empty. I go back into what used to be the office but is now the tanning facility. Steve and James are standing in front of a high-tech coffin and puzzling over the directions. They've stapled a poster of a waterfall on the wall and they are piping in some fuzzy bird chirping from the old spaghetti speakers.

You're in luck, James says. You just won a free tan.

Steve looks at James. Free? he says. Steve and James confer quietly in the corner.

I don't want a tan, I say.

Come on, man, James says. That pet store girl is crazy about guys with tans. She probably lives for the beach.

What do I do?

Lay your shit down, hombre. I'll come get you in twenty.

Could stand a little color, I guess.

That's the spirit, James says.

I strip down to my boxers and James hands me a pair of Ray Bans. I climb in and hear a switch flip and these long tubes light up. It warms quickly, and I start to think James was right about this. It's nice.

I close my eyes underneath the Ray Bans, taking in the hum of the bulbs and the bird chirping. Earlier, when we'd hit Research Library, there were six downed gate arms, none of them broken near the mechanism, so they all went in the Unusable Crate, which on one hand made our jobs easier because there was no sawing, only bolting involved, but which on the other hand always seemed needlessly wasteful to me.

We felt good about our day, like we'd worked at our useless job, until Immediate Supervisor came by to collect our Gate Arm Status Report sheets and said that there's a budget crunch, that the increased destruction of gate arms isn't helping any—so by the way we might lower the size of the Reattachment Acceptable or even duct tape some ends onto the longer Unusables. But whatever, there's a very real possibility he's going to have to let one of us go.

I have the broken gate arm radar, James immediately said.

Hey, I said. Here he was, turning it into a competition again, always at my expense. And in this case he had the edge. I had no practical skill which would give me an advantage over him in replacing gate arms. Maybe I could saw faster or bolt quicker, but probably not. If he could shave off precious seconds of the workday by driving direct to the brokens, how was I to compete?

When I wake up, there is the sense that something is wrong. The feeling of being inside the tanning machine has changed. It sears. I push the lid off the coffin and sit up. My arms, my whole body is chalky and pink. I pull on my clothes, which burn when they touch my skin.

Steve and James are leaned over the Korean Bible in the main area of the Laundromat. I come around in front of them and they don't even look until I wave a pink hand in front of the Bible.

Wait a sec, James says.

Steve points to a squiggle and tells James that it means Job.

You guys maybe forget something?

Man. You look all crabby, James says.

Timer, Steve says.

Timer, James says. Hey, we were thinking of hiring some good looking tan bitches. Maybe your girlfriend would do it?

Steve snickers.

I am standing here burnt to a crisp, I say.

You are burnt, he says. It's a significant burn, acknowledged.

Speaking of my girlfriend, we need to get ourselves to the bank, I say.

James points at another squiggle in the Bible. Steve opens up his Korean-English dictionary. Faces of the ground, Steve says.

As soon as I have time, I'm going, James says. I agreed to sign the little paper, get it witness and notarize and shit.

I say, Catch you at the schoolhouse. I take the bus home but it hurts to sit.

A cold shower brings out the red. My girlfriend rubs a special aloe cooling agent all over my body. It is one of the best nights we've shared until she boots me to the couch because, she says, I emanate too much heat. By morning I already peel.

I formulate my own proposal, looking to put me one up in the initiative category and make more work for us, which means more hours which means more payola. When Immediate Supervisor collects our Gate Arm Status Report sheets, I pose a question: Who breaks our gate arms the most, Immediate Supervisor? I say.

It's Fall, he says. Why are you so red?

Drunk people, James says.

Drunk people in cars, drunk people walking, drunk people riding bikes, Immediate Supervisor says. Students who don't want to pay. Students who want to park where they're not supposed to. Though they have universal remote openers for gate arms, emergency vehicles crash through them rather than waiting for them to rise.

There's nothing we can do about some of those, and maybe not even a freak occurrence like this Research Library thing the other day. But when mostly do all those drunks you mentioned do their damage?

Football days, he says.

Football days, I say. Of which tomorrow is one of those.

Listening, he says.

I propose that James and I, tonight and all subsequent football day eves, remove every gate arm on campus for its own protection. I believe this may be a cost-saving maneuver.

Immediate Supervisor tips his head back and mouths some numbers.

You may be onto something, he says. Do it.

So we log some overtime unbolting all sixty-nine gate arms from the mechanisms and after work, like usual, there is no time for the bank. James doesn't bring it up, and I won't bring it up. Instead we sit in the Laundromat opening and closing dryer doors, appreciating the suction of the seals, pulling out the lint screens and admiring their lack of fuzz.

Steve brings bowls of something that looks to be nipples in rice for the three of us from the Korean Grocery. The brown oblongs have little asterisks on one side. I opt out. James eats mine. He pops the things into his mouth like it's a good old time. Steve and James take 15-minute turns in the tanning machine. Their skin tones have achieved the greasy bronze of fried chicken.

I go to visit the Herp girl, who loves to pull the peeling skin from the back of my neck and feed it to the fish. She is giddy about the prospect whenever I come in. Except now, when I push through the door, she cold shoulders me. At the sight of me under the threshold of the still jingling door chimes she reaches for a small puff adder and drapes it around her neck, knowing that I won't approach her like that.

It's an interesting tongue on that necklace, I say from across the store.

She says nothing. She flips through a sea horse catalog and adjusts the puff adder. Normally a bitchy snake, known to hiss and play dead, it's nearly as calm with her as she is with it. I putter around the store, not knowing exactly what to do. I kick the side of one of the black tubs and the alligators' cat eyes meet mine.

Don't disturb them, she says. I actually have a lot of work to do today.

What work? Does any place in this strip mall besides the Korean Grocery do business?

Battery-Mart does fine, she says. Mail order is our bread and butter.

You want to feed the fish? I say, offering her my neck.

Your friend, the tan guy, was in here, she says. He told me about your girlfriend.

What girlfriend?

The one you have.

He tell you he's after her?

He told me you're on-ramp to marry.

I wouldn't say anything like that.

She puts the puff adder in its little cage. I take this as a signal, come closer.

You lied to me Broth Man, she says.

I never said anything.

Your eyes lied for you. And maybe you know a little more than I'd have a deceptor like yourself knowing. She glances at the snakehead aquarium.

Okay, I say, I get the problem here, but understand you could have been the one to break me free of her. You were the only possible chance I've seen.

You may consider yourself, as far as this store is concerned, on the illegal list henceforth. Not to be bought, sold, traded, or tampered with.

She adjusts the top of a tarantula cage, the jumper, and I back away. When the door bells jingle she is back in the sea horse catalog. I go next door and tell James I have a fucking question for him.

Well I have a fucking question for you, he says, massaging some bronzing skin cream into his forearm. Why did you do that today? It's a stupid idea.

It's a win-win.

It's no win-win. It's unnecessary. Anyone can take those gate arms off before the football games. Anyone can do that. Not just you or me. I've got us under control.

You told the Herp Girl I have a girlfriend.

Here's what you don't get, he says. I'm helping you. In every respect, I am always helping you. And it's about time you wised up to that.

The next morning we bolt on all sixty-nine gate arms, grabbing us both time-and-a-half and still saving the university over what they would have spent replacing so many. Then the very next day, on the way in, the day we're going to get to the bank and do that thing, no matter what, really, James's gate arm radar is off the charts. Could be 15, 20, he says. But when we walk into the locker room two cops are there and Immediate Supervisor with a look on his face. The cops put me and James against the lockers. Immediate Supervisor points at James and they let me go and cuff him, march him out. Immediate Supervisor tells me to go wherever it is James told me to go because gate arms are down all over campus and he should know.

They got him on felony destruction of public property, and some other things I didn't know about, vandalism, assault. They didn't even think to consider what vehicles he was driving through the gate arms, which were all stolen—mopeds, and motorcycles and a few beat-up Pontiacs. He had been coming at night all this time.

Immediate Supervisor promoted me to full-time, and I got some new responsibility for my football-day gate arm removal initiative and since there's way less gate arm work with James out of commission. Steve's Korean Laundry & Tan went out of business, and they expanded the Korean grocery into where it used to be. Now, instead of going to a Laundromat with James, me and my girlfriend sit bitterly on the porch most nights drinking margaritas and eating cold cereal with milk.

I went and visited him once. I guess it was the same old James, just something in him seemed trammeled, beaten. It made me sad to see that, because I'd always admired him for being so admirable in the way like he was above trammel or beat.

I brought him a Downy dryer sheet and he tipped his head back and laid it on his face, breathed deep for a while. It wasn't like a real jail. There was a counselor listening in. James folded the dryer sheet neatly and tucked it in his breast pocket.

At first I thought I was helping us keep our jobs, man, he said. Then I realized I couldn't stop. I had to take them out.

I told him that I understood, it was okay. A momentary look of anger flashed across his face.

They called to me in the night, he said. I shook just to approach a gate arm. They haunted my dreams.

I'm not sure if he said any of this for my benefit or the counselor's or for his own self. He confirmed once again that no matter what his circumstances, he would always have a way with the world that I would not.

Bingo

ON MY WAY TO WORK THE CAR TIRE POPS ON A
small porcupine at the curve where the kiddies speed and five
roadside crosses are maintained. I struggle a bit, flinging the
chair from the back seat, and then wheel along the shoulder
to school. A Celica pulls over and a blonde gets out. She
approaches me cautiously, cobra-like, swaying side to side. She
has what appears to be a dead koala slung off her shoulder.

"What happened, Professor?" she says.

"I've ruptured my tire on a pointed animal."

"If you'd like I can give you a ride to school. If you'd
like." She had been to my treehouse just recently with two
boys. They'd made off with the duck family, my prize. The
boys carried the mother and two ducklings. This girl picked up
the last duckling, and they all scrambled away just before Big
Daddy pulled in. Because of this I'm apprehensive. I learned
day one on this gig, you never know what the students are up

to. She's also in my fifth period, gifted.

But she's helping me into the Celica's passenger side before I've accepted the offer. She folds my chair neatly and tucks it in the trunk, ties it down with black yarn from her koala.

"I'm sorry I can't figure your name offhand?"

"Ever," she says, "It's actually Evelyn, but I'm from the South where they say it like *Everlyn*. You always call me Ms Quick in class."

She cranks the car, expertly drops it into gear, then pauses. Her hands fall into her lap and she's still, closes her eyes, then grits her teeth like an angry chimp and moans a little.

"Pardon me for a moment," she says.

"Are you okay?" I ask. She vibrates. She holds up one pulsing finger.

I adjust the seatbelt, stare straight ahead, eye her with the peripheral—her hands jumping on her knees, right foot up and down on the brake so we roll then stop, roll then stop, tipping her head back and forth in a nodding motion. I straighten the pleats in my slacks, stroke my beard. I count the reflections of my face in the cracked side view mirror, consider flinging myself out the door when the wheel rides the ditch. She shakes herself like after a good pee and apologizes, then steps off the clutch. Without even looking she swerves back onto the asphalt. She drives with the koala hanging off her shoulder.

She guns it as we race through the bends leading to school. "Again, I'm sorry about that. It's an odd thing that happens to me, the result of an unfortunate accident."

"No problem," I say.

"I'm a virgin," she says. "I swear it."

I don't say another word. Several more bends and we're

there. She helps me out, unfolds my chair, and apologizes again. I thank her and she roars off to the student parking lot.

I'm the first handicapped teacher here, and the principal installed these shoddy wooden planks as a wheelchair ramp. I engage the parking brake to not roll backwards as I open the door.

Behind his back the teachers call the principal Big Daddy because he throws his weight around. I call him Big Daddy to his face as a joke. We watch TV together at my treehouse, World Wrestling Federation, soap opera sports. He hired me on after I busted through an abortion clinic with a personalized Louisville Slugger wedding gift bat, losing my faculty job at the University, losing my legs when the abortion doctor shot me in the base of the spine to protect himself, losing the Wife because of her love for the abortionist and not for me. Yet amid local controversy the principal declared me simply the most qualified candidate to teach gifted high school health, which the state requires for graduation. He added that I was acquitted anyhow. The abortionist, in fact, dropped all charges he felt so sorry for me, which I appreciate. He didn't have to do that. So the school brought me in on one-strike-you're-out probation.

"I'm going to need your AAA," I say, slamming the office door behind me. "But let me ask you something."

"Shoot," he says. He's clicking through WWF Divas Online, one of the few pleasures of the sort he allows himself.

"This Evelyn Quick from gifted. She epileptic or something?"

"Epileptic?" he says. "No, nothing that serious. Watch out for that one."

"Watch out?"

"She seized up on you? Shook a little bit, maybe apologized?"

I nod. He hands me the AAA card.

"You want to hear a story, Professor?"

"I always want to hear a story."

"The story with her has to do with a claim. One doctor's assertion that somehow, at random...The right button in her head or something. That was his conclusion. To every second opinion, she's definitely got some misfiring synapses, but they don't even show up on the EEGs."

"What conclusion?"

"Head trauma, Professor. Claims she randomly orgasms."

"Orgasms. Can it be?"

"Can anything be? Weird on any number of levels. Now are we on for SmackDown tonight?"

You'd think the gifted kiddies would be the gift. That this would be the class teachers clamor to get. But they are the terror. This one group caused the early retirement of six teachers in the previous school year, an important reason Big Daddy was able to bring me on.

And they are clever. In the three weeks I've been here they've managed to fully uncover the circumstances about me and the by-default manner in which I came to teach them. They did not approve. They found my acre and have begun disassembling the lawn. I am powerless to stop them. The police, who are all pro-choice, think it's funny. Big Daddy thinks it's just part of what we have to put up with as teachers. *The kiddies' pranks.* It's especially cruel of him though. He knows what the lawn décor means to me. It means a lot.

The Wife and I'd started collecting them early on in the marriage. If she had a bad day, instead of bringing her flowers, I'd show up with a birdbath. When I got the flu she'd come home with a naked cupid who peed ground water. That's how it started. We went from a simple peeing naked cupid to the esoteric, the tacky, the tasteless. There's the grinning gargoyle curio shelf, a pair of flashing highway construction barrels, herds of frolicking pink-eared antelopes, lapdogs, toadstool stools, miniature horses impaled on sturdy wire from decorative pails, the obligatory herd of reindeer, and the mother duck and her ducklings which seemed entirely too wholesome for anyone to make off with. All that's left me is the grinning gargoyle, a single frolicking pink-eared antelope, and the lawn jockey.

The kiddies' methods are predictable by now. Those ornaments without any lifelikeness are simply destroyed. The birdbaths reduced to rubble, the highway barrels sawed into piles of plastic squares. But the animal-like ornaments are disappeared, replaced with fist-sized stones atop notes written in the voice of the stolen ornaments, describing why they, the ornaments, chose to leave me.

The lawn is so overgrown with grass and weeds these days the chair can't make it through. There's a path from the driveway to the treehouse elevator that's paved. But I wake up to my missing animal-like lawn ornaments replaced with notes that I can't even retrieve. So I call Big Daddy. He arrives and wades out into the yard, then reads them to me.

The duck family note read: *Dear Professor, You should know our departure has nothing to do with the weather. You might be telling yourself that we perhaps went south for the winter. This would so be wishful thinking on your part. Our intentions are 100 percent non-migratory. Our time with you has been most unpleasant. As a mother I've been embarrassed to raise children around you. You are a fowl, fowl human being. It is no wonder your wife fled. We are hastily following suit. C-ya, The Ducks.*

I ask Big Daddy to replace the notes under the appropriate stones. Sometimes the stones get turned over and the notes blow away.

When I arrive at the gifted portable the mother duck is shattered across the makeshift ramp. I recognize the feather patterns in the ceramic chips. I crunch over them as I roll up the flimsy plank into the portable.

Today's topic is Dimensions of Wellness. The diligent boy, Michael, jots notes tremendously, dabbing sweat from his forehead with the sleeve of his shirt. None of the others pay attention. Every now and then Ricky Champagne quacks softly. They forge blowguns from cafeteria straws and needles attached to spitballs. A dart barely misses my ear and sinks into a chalkboard eraser. If I maneuver nonchalantly, giving the impression I'm ignoring their attacks, they eventually get bored and turn on each other. When they aim for my head I can scratch my shoulder with my ear or my chin with my chest. But if they aim for the body, I have to be ready. The chair isn't as responsive as I'd like. So I take some hardy shots, nonchalantly.

Sure enough two of the bigger boys come forward— for a second I think they're coming for me and finger the mace in my breast pocket. But they hook their elbows underneath Michael's arms, lifting him from his desk and inserting him into the materials cabinet, locking it behind them. Then one of them chunks the keys at me. I try to dodge and they hang in my wheelchair spokes. I continue on the Wellness Continuum of Decision Making.

Their aggression is not only physical though. They are masters at psychological warfare. At the moment they are laughing about Michael, scrawling love insignias on notebooks, reaching their grubby hands through the holes in the backs of chairs. I try to regain whatever authority I ever had by describing the four dimensions of wellness: Physical (proper nutrition, exercise, avoiding harmful substances), Intellectual (gathering information, problem solving), Emotional (self-control, enthusiasm for life, high self-esteem), and Social (making friends, cooperating, being a productive member of society). But none of them are listening.

Ricky Champagne shouts out "Leg" and the entire class goes silent. For a second, thrown out there like that, the word disorients them. But their painful, wide-eyed stares drop to my leg, which still gets the twitches even though I don't feel below the waist. I'm confused myself. It's a part of me I don't consider even. But Ricky Champagne's accusatory shout-out to my anatomy causes me, the whole class in fact, to consider it. I look down at the leg, which is ever so slightly pulsing. Then I look up again and they're all caught up with it, blank-faced, open-mouthed enchantment. The word hanging in the air like that leaves them no choice.

In back, Ever pulls tacks from the bulletin board and gnaws on them. She vibrates occasionally and looks around to see if anyone notices.

The rest of them are fixated on my leg, which is pathetically skinny, devoid of muscle. The cuff of my pant leg crooked, revealing a dirty white sock, underneath a bald cream shin peers out. I fix the cuff then animate furiously, turning circles in the chair, trying to divert their attention.

But they're ready for me. "Hand," another boy shouts when I scrawl wellness charts on the chalkboard. Then they all stare at my hand. A small liver spot—my first—underneath the big knuckle. The skin is wrinkled like when you straighten out a crumpled sheet of paper. I shake the hand and move it around. Their eyes follow. My hand trembles a tiny bit. I write to keep it in check, "For tomorrow PP. 120-162, Defense Mechanisms: Repression, Rationalization, Compensation, Projection, Idealization, Daydreaming, Regression, Denial, Sublimation, Displacement, Reaction Formation, Negativism..." My hand jumps, scraggly, incomplete lines. I hold it in front of my face and peer through my fingers at the class, still transfixed, as if my hand was some *thing* they'd never seen before.

The bell rings, breaking the spell. The sound of the word "Hand" is replaced with the sound of zippers on backpacks, shuffling papers, sneakers on the tile floor.

"Bye, Professor Crazier-than-a-Shithouse-Rat," Ricky Champagne says.

When he and the bigger boys are gone I let Michael out. He thanks me and copies the assignment off the board, looking back at my leg as he leaves, then at my hand, then at my face. I wheel myself to the faculty lounge, where the walkways are too narrow for what the insurance company calls my "personal transportation vehicle." No one will open the door for me in the teacher lounge even though I can hear voices: the gifted language arts teacher says to another teacher, "You want to hear what this little bastard said to me? He goes, 'If you can tell the meaning of the word from the context, then why do you need the word?'"

The only things worse than the kiddies are the red squirrels. They stalk me like the kiddies do, up into the tree. And this treehouse isn't your ordinary thing. I built it myself in the oaks right around the time I found out about the Wife's affair with the abortionist. I slept here when she didn't come home and I could walk. It has outlets, insulation, running water, an electric platform elevator that operates on pulleys, brown carpet, and several pump pellet rifles. Once I got out of the hospital with the handicap, being alone in the house was intolerable, so I started coming up here again. It was in part a penance. It made life more difficult and kept me in constant jeopardy. Now the electricity is shut off in the main house. The doorways there aren't big enough for the chair and the carpet is impossible to wheel through.

Everything there reminds me of her.

We started off with normal gray squirrels. They were almost tame, cute, their numbers slim. Before she left, I bought the Wife the Holy Grail of yard décor, interactive yard décor at that, a device resembling a little windmill with pegs on the ends to which she'd attach corncobs smothered in peanut butter. Attach that whole apparatus to a tree and the gray squirrels would tip back on their hind legs respectably, spin the mill until they got hold of a cob, clean the kernels of peanut butter, then drop the rest for the birds. Sometimes they slipped and clung to a rotating cob and me and the Wife would laugh, mauling grapefruits on the back porch. I don't know where the red squirrels came from but they started showing up one day. They kept the gray ones at bay. They're smaller than the gray squirrels, with white spots on their chests. These red squirrels took flight from faraway tree limbs and pounced. They held tight and ate peanut butter, kernel, cob, everything, and the Wife and I admired their determination and vigor.

But the red squirrels kept multiplying. Our yard, trees, ornaments, everything overrun with them. They chased away the timid gray squirrels. They evicted the birds from the birdbaths. They nested in the grinning gargoyle curio shelf. And one day we retired the mill when a red squirrel leapt from an overhead limb and bit the Wife.

But they'd moved in for good. Now they burrow their way into the wood of the treehouse. They store nuts and moss there. They mate and fight on the roof at night. They squeeze in under the windows and deposit squirrel shit in the carpet. The pellet guns are for them.

Big Daddy and I meet AAA then he follows me to the treehouse. I'm relieved. His car in the driveway is enough to keep the kiddies away. At home my four garage windows are busted and two red squirrels dart in and out in a game of chase. I lunge for one as it scurries by, forgetting for a moment that I can't walk. The Principal rights me, and we adjourn to the treehouse for SmackDown.

"They trespass everything," I blubber, gauging the patter of small feet in the tree. I try to get into the match, but the sound of their ratty feet in the tree just has me going tonight.

"Thank God for this sport," the Principal says.

"I'll take these rodents from beneath," says I, grabbing a pellet gun and wheeling toward the elevator.

"I'll keep you posted," the Principal says.

On the ground I take aim at anything red that moves, but my pellets suck dirt. Then I pump the thing up again. It's supposed to be twenty-pump, but I can barely get past five. You'd think my arms would be stronger wheeling around all the time but it's the opposite.

Ever steps out from the trunk like a tree sprite and almost gets shot. She hands me the last duckling, unharmed. She plops to the ground, drawing her knees up close and binding them in her arms. She flicks her earring and taps the koala backpack in her lap. I rest the rifle across my armrests.

"You're the only teacher to know, you know," she says. "Besides who's-his-face up there. Whatcha think?"

"I think your situation is unfortunate," I say.

"There's lots of things I miss about being normal," she says.

"What are you doing here, Ms Quick?"

"It's Ever," she says. "I wanted to apologize."

"For what? You helped me today."

"For when I was here with those boys. They found out where you lived from the auditor's website," she says. She explains that she's seldom asked to go along on anything.

The Principal hollers: "Annihilate the bastards, Champion! The Rock's in the middle of his speech, and they're munching through the wires." Ever looks up.

"You better go now," I say.

"Okay."

"Thanks for bringing it back," I say.

Back upstairs I prop the pellet gun against Big Daddy's recliner. The duckling goes on top of the TV. "Did you hit any of them?" he says.

"I'm a lousy shot," I say, as the electricity flickers, then goes out.

Big Daddy is called out of our lunch when another student wrecks at the curve in the road. It interrupts the liverwurst and mustard sandwiches made for us by the secretaries, Gerald and Gerard. They're old men, gay and living together though me and Big Daddy are the only ones to know. They somehow got in the habit of fixing us lunch every day because we are very old helpless men and they are slightly younger old helpless men. They keep a small radio in the main office constantly tuned to the Christian rock station.

With Big Daddy gone, I filter through the files. Evelyn Marquee Quick. 162 IQ. Family from Sewanee. Never received a grade below A in her entire academic history. But last year, an odd blip on the medical records. She was absent from school for a solid two months. I can make out "bingo accident" on the doctor notes, but the absentee forms are blotted out, ripped, damaged beyond readability. I hear steps outside the office, stick the file back into place, and roll back to my liverwurst as Gerard pops his head in the door.

"No fatalities," he says. "Damn the Jaws of Life."

Well, the accident just served to rile them up. When it comes time for my class they are heaving textbooks at walls, and rolling small nails under my wheels. I'm talking techniques for managing stress: "Visualization. Deliberate daydreaming about pleasant surroundings. A defense mechanism." Ricky Champagne's eyes feast on me. I can see right through to his little brain, pondering my physicality, searching for just the right part. I glance down at myself as well, practice standard defensive body language, arms folded across the chest.

"Crotch," he announces.

And Ever spits a tack. "Why don't you just shut up, Rick Champagne. Everyone knows *you're* nothing but a hyperactive, pre-pubescent, bald-pecker hormone cluster and no one's all that impressed."

The class goes silent, but now they consider him. He tries to come at me again, though by less clever means. "You're saying it's healthful to daydream? This is whacked, everyone knows only freaks sit around daydreaming all day. Or those whose lives are so miserable due to their own stupid actions they have no choice but to daydream." He chuckles, implies me, looks around the room for support.

Ever stares him down. She shakes her head slowly then reverts attention to the front. Everyone else follows suit. It is the first time I understand her power, whether the orgasms are real or not. How her peers must be scared of her and in awe of her. How their barely pubescent minds can't comprehend her. How the mystery of the female orgasm must seem so clear to her. How some women go their whole lives without even one and this girl has multiples every day that seize her foundation.

Ricky Champagne straightens up in his chair. Then he bolts, bawling and blubbering like a kindergartner, out the classroom door.

I capitalize quickly and get through like three days' lessons in one 50-minute period. It's amazing. I teach again. Health is all of a sudden a magical thing. Their eyes glitter with recognition. Some of them write notes. When the bell rings they wait for me to dismiss them before packing up. I say, "You're dismissed."

Then I say, "Hold on a minute, Ever."

Michael stops on his way out the door. He's always the last one to leave class, generally after my releasing him from some sort of confinement, so he feels uncomfortable. He looks from Ever to me. "Fascinating stuff this Immune Response Mobilization, Professor," he says. "Would you be able to explain to me again the communication between the helper T cell and the B cell?"

"Let's talk about that tomorrow, Michael," I say. He nods, shuffles. Looking back as if betrayed, he slides out the door.

"Yes, Professor?" she says.

"Why did you do that?" I say.

"You're welcome," she says.

"Well thanks," I say. "I owe you twice."

"Hold on," she says, reaching out and taking both my wrists in her hands. She looks into my face. I look down at her white knuckles. She shakes.

"Ever," I say, "Are you faking these?"

Her eyes are like drops of mud. She tightens her grip. "It starts around the baby thing, then shoots all through me."

The electrician explains to me that, indeed, small rodents apparently chewed through the treehouse's electric wires. Though he doesn't know how they managed that without barbequing themselves. Then we locate a formerly red now charcoal squirrel at the bottom of the tree. "Guess they couldn't," the electrician says, laughing. He goes to his truck and comes back with a Miracle Whip jar filled with powder. A strip of tape across the top reads "Strychnine."

"This prevents recurrences," he says. "And I don't have to honor no guarantee."

I thank him. He patches the wires up and leaves. Then I bring out the Wife's old mill. Attach juicy cobs of sweet corn to it and coat them with extra crunchy peanut butter and a sprinkling of strychnine. This is the difference between the kiddies and the red squirrels. The kiddies are way too smart to fall for this. But the red squirrels come right away.

I park the chair on the porch and eat a grapefruit like me and the Wife used to. In no time at all they wretch and plunge from the tree. It reminds me of a time when Big Daddy and I were merely acquaintances, former classmates. He was just a guy who answered the phone at the high school when I wanted to go out for beers. Standing, I was taller than a lot of tall people.

The squirrels crawl and writhe through the weeds. Their filthy red bodies flip around. They crawl toward the little rocks where the lawn ornaments used to be like they're crawling toward their pitiful little tombstones. I chunk the grapefruit rind and hit one on the head. They squirm until I almost can't take the joy anymore. And finally, almost all at once, they're still.

Two Hours and Fifty-three Minutes

From: WheelerDealer@yahoo.com
Date: Wednesday, November 22, 2006 11:42 AM
To: jnotice@moose-mail.com
Subject: a little catch-up

Dear Jana,

Hi, I found your address online. It might be weird to get an email from me after so long.

I don't rightly know where to begin. I often remember those days in '94 and '95: You and I, two spry young HTML coders who couldn't get enough of each other. What really did it for me was how you brought our work back to the bedroom. Serious. I loved that. If you had been one of those "Fuck me with your big dick" kind of girls, I don't think we would have made it as long as we did. But there was this one thing you would scream—I can hear your voice right now: "Open carrot, div, align equals right, close carrot, indention, open carrot, image, space, source equals harder dot harder dot harder dot jpeg, close carrot, indent out, open carrot, backslash, div, close carrot." I couldn't control myself. And you didn't have to worry about referring to external javascripts or style sheets or database query strings which is what it's all about now, so technified and unerotic. Those days, the early days of the Internet, were much simpler times. Give me a basic scripting language over object orientation any day.

I should probably give you the old me-update huh? I kept on with the coding, moving up here and there as the technology changed. Eventually I bought a book on SQL and learned databases. It was a good move at a good time from a career perspective. The past five years I've been in database design. It's interesting, when you're building databases all day you focus in on one thing, the primary key. Everything else is relation, relation, relation. Does this other thing relate to my primary key? If so, how? If not, how to organize the relation?

It's not the reason I'm writing. My wife—yeppers, married—wants to have a baby. We've been trying for a while and with no results. I suggested she get a fertility check up and she kind of half got offended. Ah, that's not true. Lisa doesn't get offended. Everything is ironic with her. But she got ironic offended and said I needed to get a fertility check up too. I said, "Look, it's not me okay. I've been responsible for two abortions in my life." Lisa thinks this is a trip. She accuses me of bragging about my abortions. But I'm a good sport and I went and did the jerk off into a cup thing. The results came back showing her pond fully stocked. Me? Low sperm motility, which means the percentage of moving sperm and their quality of motion. I'm telling them that their results must be off, to retest, and they say things like, it's not the first time they've had a guy who can't make babies suggest a history with a woman who claimed they made a baby. I about punched him for, in effect, calling into question your good name—you know how fond I've always been of you, Jana, even after we split. I checked around on the Internet and certain people's sperm motility does decrease over time, especially if they're mountain bikers or some new studies show that cell phones actually have an impact. But I don't ride and I don't talk so much on the cell, surely not enough for that. Quite the opposite. I sit ten-hour days in a one-thousand dollar ergonomically correct office chair, comfortably resting my balls on an indentation which keeps them, as I code, warm and balanced.

Sometimes things seem so far away though it's like you don't really even remember them. You can start to feel crazy because part of you is so sure your life went like this and another part of you feels this panic because maybe you misread something all these years. I don't know what I'm really trying to get at. I just think about you sometimes, especially when something like this comes up. I hope it doesn't create bad memories or something. Where are you in the world?

Solid Gold,

Dealer

From: jnotice@moose-mail.com
Date: Wednesday, November 22, 2006 12:14 PM
To: WheelerDealer@yahoo.com
Subject: Re: a little catch-up

Dealer,

Conceivably it'd be nice to hear from you. But do you have to be so pornographic? I'm not like that anymore. Let's agree to keep this brief electronic reunion strictly business. You wrote me for a reason and I'll discuss that point with you because it's having some bearing on your life, which I don't feel completely comfortable about. (But I'm not accepting your friend request on MySpace, and you really should write people before just adding them.)

There's something I never told you. I came down with a condition while we were together. It's kind of rare, often misdiagnosed, leads to all kinds of break-ups, divorces, single-parent children, lifelong sex phobias, blah blah blah. So the fallout in our situation pales totally in comparison. We hardly even knew each other.

The fact is, I was never pregnant. It was a ridiculous excuse to keep from having sex with you, because of this condition, because I started getting headaches when we did it. At first I thought what was causing the headaches was the screaming. I always hated HTML. I did that for you, because I very well knew you loved it. If I have a gift it's knowing what people love. It's called Sexual Headache and means a sudden, excruciating headache when approaching orgasm and afterward.

It's actually dangerous. Women have ruptured cerebral blood vessels.

I was stupid and insecure. I didn't want to tell you I was getting headaches. I thought you'd hate me. On top of that the old sex-headache cliché. So I told you I was pregnant. I invented the abortion saga, carried it out for months. Those times I wept, it was because I was imbalanced. I began to hate me and to hate you. The doctor told me it was impossible to tell what caused Sexual Headache, but that he was sure if I didn't have sex, it would solve the problem. The abortion story bought me time. When you dropped me off that day, why do you think I ordered you not to come in? I had scheduled a routine exam, a consultation on birth control. That took about twenty minutes, and I sat in the waiting room while you sat in the parking lot until I figured I'd sat roughly long enough to have an abortion and walk away from it.

Remember that one fight, when I screamed, "I can't live with what we've done"? That's the part I regret. That lie. In truth I couldn't live with the headache I got while we were doing it. And the thing is, I'm grateful for all of it. I didn't have the strength to break up with you otherwise. I didn't have sex with anyone for more than a year, but when I did, it was fine, great even—and no headache. It never occurred again. The cause of my Sexual Headache was you.

I don't want to seem heartless, Dealer. I do have nice memories of you. But honestly, the capillaries in my brain feel constricted just emailing you. I'm sorry to hear about your motility and I wish you and what's-her-name the best of luck, but don't write again.

Jana

From: WheelerDealer@yahoo.com
Date: Wednesday, November 22, 2006 12:16 PM
To: jnotice@moose-mail.com
Subject: Re: Re: a little catch-up

You always were a neurotic bitch. Thanks for fucking out my world.

From: WheelerDealer@yahoo.com
Date: Wednesday, November 22, 2006 12:20 PM
To: KkrazychickK@gmail.com
Subject: quick question

Dear KkrazychickK,

Hey. Nice email handle. It's got great symmetry. So yeah, this is Dealer. It's been a while huh? I tracked you down online. Looks like you're working for some yoga place—sounds hot!

To be honest I'm in a bit of a panic here. I'll give you the condensed version: my new wife—yeppers, married—wants to have kids. We haven't used protection in years because

I guess you could say we were never really not trying. I assumed the reason nothing ever happened in the kid way was that she couldn't have children. This made sense to me in terms of karma, that I would fall in love with a woman who couldn't conceive. I figured I'd aborted my chances at children and now by the natural laws of the universe, I would not have them. I remember the abortion you had when we were together. That really broke me up. The funny thing is, I've been diagnosed with low sperm motility. In other words, my boys lack *oomph*. But I'm trying to figure out if this is something that's happened over time, or if it's always been this way. Obviously, it can't be the latter, because you got pregnant when we were together. We had that little scare afterward, with the blood in the toilet. And you called the doctor and it was just a normal clot. I know this must seem weird and probably unpleasant. I'm just trying to clarify. I've had some disturbing revelations of late.

Hope everything's okay in your life and in your bidniss.

Solid Gold,

Dealer

From: KkrazychickK@gmail.com
Date: Wednesday, November 22, 2006 01:07 PM
To: WheelerDealer@yahoo.com
Subject: Re: quick question

Hey you, that's so strange. I was just thinking about you the other day. The owner of a studio I work at was interested in building a database of her clients and asked me if I knew anyone who did that stuff. I said that I did but I hadn't talked to him in a few years.

I'm teaching Pilates and Bikram Yoga at a few places in Oakland. Do you know what Bikram is? It's like hot yoga. So, yeah, it is hot, about 106 degrees to be exact. The poses are designed to tourniquet your body with long, low-impact stretches, which you hold, cutting off the blood flow, then release, and your blood surges through you again, rushing oxygen to every tissue. It's the life. Nothing but good feeling from me. You're probably right about the karma. I don't want kids. You'll think I'm crazy. I have four dogs: a great dane, a pug, some kind of dalmation mix and a shmorkie-poo.

Listen, about that abortion back then, I've got to be honest with you. I wish I'd known how to get in touch with you because I've needed to for a while about this very thing. I ended up in a twelve-step program not long after we split. I had it coming even then. One of the steps was to apologize to everyone you had hurt and/or lied to in one way or another. You were at the top of my Had Lied To list. I was cheating on you with four or five guys. You tended to use condoms whereas they didn't. So I doubt it was yours. In fact I can say almost for sure, I doubt it was yours. I know whose it was. I remember exactly when it happened. You would have been at work, which is when I would meet with this particular one. It happened just like I always imagined it would, mystically, under a tree, in the rain. But it wasn't you. You were the only one who stepped up to the plate though. I figured because you had experience from that other girl, the one you got pregnant before me. You knew how to deal with things. Good because I didn't want to have anything to do with that guy. You were really sweet during all of that. I'd like to send you the money you paid for it. What was it, like 400 dollars? What's your address?

Kisses,

Kim

From: WheelerDealer@yahoo.com
Date: Wednesday, November 22, 2006 01:09 PM
To: KkrazychickK@gmail.com
Subject: Re: Re: quick question

You've got to be kidding me. Four or five guys? Under a tree? In the rain? Are you sure that wasn't a movie? Or maybe you're misremembering. Time is like that sometimes. Especially with all the pills you were doing.

The database stuff isn't hard to learn. Well, I take that back, the query languages take some time, but the actual design of the database is pretty simple. You have a number of entities with different sets of data, but each entity shares one thing in common. That's your primary key, which forces entity integrity by uniquely identifying entity instances. Then there's your foreign key, which enforces referential integrity by completing an association between two entities. These keys can be as meaningless as an ID number or meaningful, like a last name.

I am still trying to picture this: you under a tree in the rain, being mystically impregnated by one of four or five men you are sleeping with during the time I am at the office learning the principle of the primary key. You could say that I feel right now like the keys of my life have just been blipped. It's primary key rule numero uno, that each instance of its entity must have a non-null value. When it's pulled out from under you, it's a crusher.

Pilates and Yoga? You must be in great shape. Could you send me a pic? Are you born again and everything now?

Solid Gold,

Dealer

From: KkrazychickK@gmail.com
Date: Wednesday, November 22, 2006 01:35 PM
To: WheelerDealer@yahoo.com
Subject: Re: Re: Re: quick question

Yes, it's what happened. Time I'm very clear on. The mistakes add up quick.

I know in my heart that there's something out there, Wheeler, something governing the universe. But I don't believe in God. I didn't fall for that part of it. I only fell for the part that could help me. It's not selfishness though. I know in my heart by helping me it helps the rest of the world too. I was corrosive before. Now I am galvanic.

I don't get any of what you said about keys.

Seriously, send me your address. I'm waiting. Atonement, at last…

Kim

ps: Here's a shot they took for my instructor profile. It's the Sasangasana, the rabbit pose. I can do that shit all day long.

From: WheelerDealer@yahoo.com
Date: Wednesday, November 22, 2006 01:38 PM
To: KkrazychickK@gmail.com
Subject: getting over it already

Wow. You look totally collapsed in on yourself there. I mean, it's a good look for you. I think I can safely say you are the hottest woman I ever went out with. You were probably my best chance at natural selection. Of course back then you were so fucked up it probably would have been the village idiot. But present wife included, you are definitely the hottest. That's no dis to Lisa. Lisa is amazing. She's totally ironic, and she just deflects things. And she'll try anything but in moderation. I think she knew all along that it was me, that I was the problem. And she let me blather on about my abortions and how it had to be her. I'm still fucked over all of this. Did you ever have dreams about the kid, Kim? I have dreams about the kid all the time, and not only that one. I dream about the other one I supposedly (don't get me started) aborted with that neurotic bitch. I've had such vivid dreams I woke up in the morning and thought I heard the both of them, two boys, chattering away downstairs in front of the TV. They'd be five and eight now if they ever really existed. It never bothered me. Never. Not until now. I carried them with me and that was enough, and now I find out I was carrying nothing all along. It's like the opposite of that Jesus-and-footprints-in-the-sand story. You don't think something like that will affect you, but it does. It affects you.

Solid Gold,

Dealer

From: WheelerDealer@yahoo.com
Date: Wednesday, November 22, 2006 02:10 PM
To: KkrazychickK@gmail.com
Subject: indecent proposal

What does a guy have to do to get an invite to the Bay Area and a complimentary body tourniquet?

From: WheelerDealer@yahoo.com
Date: Wednesday, November 22, 2006 02:20 PM
To: gogogadgetsoul@gmail.com
Subject: where we stand

Well, babe, I've been searching for answers. Things are confirmed: I was a dope, duped. My boys never swam, Lisa. I hereby drop my claims on the good people at Fertilocertainty. I hereby restore their good name. My abortions were fictions all these years. Those cunts. I could understand one, but two? Where do you find girls like that? It's been a grand deception. I just thought of something funny, babe: False sense of sterility. But that's not quite it, is it?

Solid Gold,

Your Deal

From: gogogadgetsoul@gmail.com
Date: Wednesday, November 22, 2006 2:35 PM
To: WheelerDealer@yahoo.com
Subject: Re: where we stand

Dealer,

I'll see you tonight. We'll make it. There are drugs to teach your boys to swim or technologies to do the swimming for them. And in the end, it's just another project of mine. If it doesn't work out, I'll find another project. This is how well I understand me. The ROOMBA robotic vacuum is already tempting. It's like a puppy except instead of shitting and pissing all over the place, it cleans. It's cute, adorable even, a little toaster-sized cross between Knight Rider and R2-D2. Don't worry about your ex-cunts. I'm more than you could ever ask for.

xo,

Lisa

Notes

"False Cognate" – The quotation about Black Widow suicide bombers is adapted from *The New York Times*, "Female Suicide Bombers Unnerve Russians," August 7, 2003.

"An Evening of Jenga®" owes acknowledgements to the Gordon Lish-edited version of Raymond Carver's story "What We Talk About When We Talk About Love" and to the Milton Bradley Company.

"The Taste of Penny" – The quotations used in Jeremy's call out to the Two Men And A Truck crew are from, respectively, *David Copperfield* by Charles Dickens; *Wilhelm Meister's Apprenticeship* by J.W. von Goethe; and the poem "An Epilogue at Wallack's" by John Elton Wayland.

Acknowledgments

Thanks to all the journal and anthology editors who first published these stories.

I stole material for many of them. Thanks to Tom Burke, Nathan Deuel, Elizabeth Ellen, Kevin Keck, and Tony Walsch for being agreeable victims.

These stories have been a long time coming and many have had my back along the way, sometimes without even knowing. Thanks to Aaron Burch, JJ Butts, Mary Caponegro, Igor Chesnokov, Tony Earley, Jon Fink, Arthur Flowers, the folks, John Goldbach, Mikhail Iossel, Josh Knelman, Phil LaMarche, Adam Levin, Mima, my wife, Natural Light, Jason Ockert, Robert Olmstead, Crystal Parker, Tiffany Parker, Padgett Powell, Russki Standart, George Saunders, the Sewanee Writer's Conference, Briggs Seekins, Meg Storey, and Ashley Vaught.

Special thanks to the Croatian Sensation Josip Novakovich.

Another special thanks to Stephen Lyons and John Jenkins at DECODE for publishing the limited edition chapbook *The Back of the Line* with images by my man/genius William Powhida, which make the James stories much better. (More info on that can be found at http://www.decodebooks.com/bookstore.html.)

As always, thanks to Ellen Levine.

And finally thanks to everyone at Dzanc Books, designer Steven Seighman for taping flyers to a telephone pole, Mary Gillis for copyediting, and especially Steve Gillis and Dan Wickett. Most publishers are content that the work they publish is impact on the world enough. Dzanc ups the ante, giving to kids and the incarcerated and more. It's an honor to be associated with them.